GUARDIAN

GALACTIC GLADIATORS #9

ANNA HACKETT

Guardian

Published by Anna Hackett

Copyright 2018 by Anna Hackett

Cover by Melody Simmons of eBookindiecovers

Edits by Tanya Saari

ISBN (ebook): 978-1-925539-43-1

ISBN (paperback): 978-1-925539-44-8

Hell Squad – Amazon Bestselling Science Fiction Romance Series and SFR Galaxy Award for best Post-Apocalypse for Readers who don't like Post-Apocalypse

The Anomaly Series – #1 Amazon Action Adventure Romance Bestseller

"Like Indiana Jones meets Star Wars. A treasure hunt with a steamy romance." – SFF Dragon, review of *Among Galactic Ruins*

"Strap in, enjoy the heat of romance and the daring of this group of space travellers!" – Di, Top 500 Amazon Reviewer, review of *At Star's End*

"Action, danger, aliens, romance – yup, it's another great book from Anna Hackett!" – Book Gannet Reviews, review of *Hell Squad: Marcus*

Sign up for my VIP mailing list and get your *free box set* containing three action-packed romances.

Visit here to get started:
www.annahackettbooks.com

CHAPTER ONE

S he pushed for more speed.

Dayna Caplan's feet slapped on the fancy alien version of a treadmill. Her lungs were burning as she ran, her arms pumping, and sweat sheened her face. She touched the controls, unable to read most of the strange alien text, but the treadmill incline rose another degree and the speed increased.

Perfect. She ran harder, pushing herself to the limit. She loved feeling her muscles warm and limber. Most of all, she liked being free.

No more cells. No more screams. No more fights to the death. No more pain.

She kept running, sweat pouring into her eyes. When her legs threatened to give out, she finally touched the button to end the program. When she stepped off, her legs rubbery, she pulled in some deep breaths. Her gaze moved to the floor-to-ceiling windows that ringed the gym, located on the uppermost level of the Dark Nebula Casino.

A hell of a view. The city spread out as far as she could see, until it met the desert in the distance. Two large suns sat high in the sky, like large orange balloons.

Not New York. Her throat tightened. Not even her planet. This was Kor Magna. An alien city on the wild desert planet of Carthago, half a galaxy away from Earth. Her gaze fell on the circular stone shape of the Kor Magna Arena—home to the gladiatorial houses and the fights that the city was famous for.

Her hands clenched into painful balls. She'd been abducted by Thraxian slavers, and subjected to captivity on this lawless desert planet on the galaxy's outer rim. Two other women were still trapped at the vicious desert arena of Zaabha—Ever and Sam. Dayna didn't know them, but she knew exactly what they were suffering.

With a bad taste filling her throat, she strode across the high-tech gym. She grabbed the ropes on a machine and started bicep curls. The machine calibrated to her strength automatically, increasing the resistance.

She wasn't at Zaabha anymore. Her captivity at the desert arena had ended when she'd been sold to a desert witch who'd thrived on pain. Still lifting, Dayna looked down at her leggings and fitted top. She couldn't see through the black fabric, but she knew what she'd find. She swallowed. She'd been at the Dark Nebula for two weeks, and she'd spent it working her butt off to get her strength and health back.

Because she couldn't help free Sam and Ever if she was weak.

Releasing the ropes, she gripped the hem of her workout shirt and lifted it up. Her belly looked as it always had—not flat, but toned from her regular workouts. But as she lifted the fabric higher, the horrible taste in her throat increased. There, resting in the center of her chest, just below her breasts, she saw what looked like an amber stone embedded in her skin.

She closed her eyes and her stomach rolled. She stared the truth in the face. An alien symbiont was living inside her.

Dayna sucked in some deep breaths. As a New York City police detective, she'd been known for being level-headed, okay, and sometimes hard-headed, but she was always a problem solver. She *would* find a way to deal with this.

Dropping her shirt, she faced the windows again. She pressed a hand to the glass, looking past the city of Kor Magna and to the desert beyond.

There was no way home. No way back to Earth. And there was no way to remove the *thing* living inside her.

Pain sliced at her. Pain for the familiar home she'd known, for her grief-stricken father who'd lost the last member of his family.

The stone flashed through her shirt, as if the creature inside her was responding to her emotions.

Gritting her teeth, Dayna forced herself to relax. *Calm down. Focus on the facts.* Even if there were a ship fast enough, she and the other people who'd been abducted from a space station orbiting Jupiter couldn't leave Carthago. Earth was too far away and the wormhole the Thraxians had used was gone. There was no way

3

home, and even if a wormhole appeared tomorrow, there was no going home for her. She gingerly touched the stone under her shirt and knew that she would never be the same again. Forever, she'd be linked to a creature about the size of her hand nestled in her chest.

Panic skittered up her spine and she ruthlessly shoved it away. She'd felt this same drowning helplessness once before...when her sister had been kidnapped as a child.

No. She straightened. She wasn't a whiner or a quitter. They hadn't called her Bulldog Caplan at the precinct because she sat around wallowing. Dayna Katherine Caplan was made of stronger stuff.

She started some lunges, working out until her thighs burned. She was back to her pre-abduction weight and she was even stronger than she had been before. It was time. She couldn't just sit around working out, lazing in the giant tub in the bathroom off the gorgeous bedroom she'd been given, or even wandering the casino, as had become her habit since she'd been able to get out of bed.

She needed to help find Zaabha. She *needed* to help rescue Sam and Ever.

Taking a moment to blot her face with a towel, she then retied her hair, pulling the thick brown mass back in a ponytail. Then she headed out of the gym, purpose riding her.

As she walked down the corridor, her workout shoes squeaking on the polished floor, she heard his voice.

Her steps slowed and she let the deep, masculine drawl wash over her.

The man had a hell of a voice. It was one that made a

woman think of dark nights, silken sheets, and decadent pleasure.

She snorted to herself. *Get a grip, Caplan.* The man was clearly on a business call, and the last thing she needed was to be thinking anything sexual about the man who'd given her sanctuary.

The glossy double doors at the end of the hall were open and she paused in the doorway.

Okay, she took back her last thought. Any woman, from any planet, couldn't look at Rillian—owner of the most profitable casino in Kor Magna, and who knew what else—and not think of sex.

He was standing at the windows, his back to her, and his long, lean form silhouetted by the light. Dark trousers made of a fine fabric encased narrow hips and long legs. His jacket was tossed over a chair by his huge desk and his snowy white shirt contrasted against bronze skin. Black, silky hair fell to his shoulders.

She hadn't made a sound, but he sensed her and turned. God, that face. Too dangerous for a movie star, too sexy for even a fallen angel. The top few buttons of his white shirt were undone, baring his throat and a triangle of delectable skin. He wore some sort of earpiece in his right ear.

"I want you to put pressure on the investors of the Dark Oasis Project to make their commitments. I've given them plenty of time to think about it. I want to break ground on this development next week." He paused, waving Dayna inside. "Yes, next week, Londo. Make it happen."

As she moved across his palatial office, she tried to

ignore the way his silver gaze stayed on her. After two weeks of living with him, she was well aware that Rillian didn't miss a thing.

Since her rescue from the desert witch who'd shoved the symbiont in Dayna, Mr. Wealthy-and-Mysterious had become her guardian. Or perhaps prison warden was a better description.

"Hi." Damn, she wished she'd showered and changed before coming to see him. She felt like she'd dragged herself out of a gutter while he was all polished and tailored.

"Good afternoon." He walked over to a long built-in cabinet. His body blocked her view, but when he turned back to her, he held out an icy glass of water. "Drink."

Damn man was always feeding her or getting her to drink something. She took the glass with a roll of her eyes.

"You've been in the gym again." His gaze swept over her workout gear.

His eyes were a strange mix of silver and black, and were constantly changing. Sometimes they were all silver, sometimes black with sparks of silver in them like lightning, and always fascinating.

"Not overdoing it, I hope."

"No, mom. I'm following all the healer's orders." She drank some of the cool water, then set the glass on his desk. "I'm feeling really good, Rillian. I..." She straightened. "I'm going crazy."

He cocked his head. "You're bored? I've provided you with everything I thought you might need. A well-appointed room, adjoining gym, entertainment screens, full run of the casino—"

"I'm not saying my room isn't the most opulent, gorgeous room I've ever stayed in." She shoved her hair back over her shoulder. "But I can't laze around when I know Ever and Sam are out there. Suffering."

Rillian slid his hands into his pockets. "The House of Galen is doing everything they can to find the women."

She knew that the gladiators who'd taken in the rest of the human survivors were working hard and were just as worried as she was. She'd spoken a few times with some of the other women, mostly her closest friends, Mia and Winter. Or rather, the pair constantly called her, demanding to know how she was doing.

"I know the gladiators and the other women from Earth are doing everything possible," Dayna said. "But...I have to do something. I *need* to do something."

"You need to recover—"

She threw her arms out. "I'm recovered."

That silver gaze ran over her again and Dayna felt it, like a visceral punch to her belly. She forced herself to stay still. She needed sexual attraction in her chaotic life right now as much as she needed a hole in the head.

"And your symbiont?" he asked silkily. "How are you doing with that?"

Her jaw locked and her chest tightened. "Fine."

"You haven't fed it yet."

"I'm not a *parasite*," she hissed.

He sighed. "Until you come to terms with—"

She spun away. "I read the information you gave me on the symbiont, about it requiring biological energy, but I don't want to talk about it. Right now, Ever and Sam are what matter. I need to help them."

Silence stretched in the room. God, how could she make him see how important this was to her without showing him all her weaknesses? The man was all cool, suave control, and he'd already seen her at her worst so many times. Wasn't she allowed to keep a scrap of her pride?

"I'll have Tannon provide you with all the data we have on the search for Zaabha."

At Rillian's words, she spun, her shoulders relaxing. "Thank you." She cleared her throat. "You probably already know this, but your head of security doesn't like me."

Rillian smiled. "I pay Tannon very well to be paranoid and suspicious."

She pulled a face. "Well, he's good at it. I mean it, thank you for helping me do this."

That gaze was on her again, like he could see right into her. She felt a tug in her belly and squelched it. Okay, tried to squelch it. She couldn't remember the last time she'd had sex and Rillian was just far too potent to ignore.

"You're welcome, Dayna. Anything you need, I'll get it for you."

Instantly, the image of Rillian's long-fingered hands moving over her heated skin popped into her head. *Dammit.*

He stepped in front of her, his scent hitting her. Something dark and spicy.

"I'll let you know when Tannon's put together the data."

She nodded. Dayna wasn't too proud to admit that

she needed to escape Rillian's presence and regroup. "Thanks again." She headed for the door.

"Dayna, one more thing."

She looked back over her shoulder.

"You can't ignore your symbiont. When you're ready, I'm here to help." Silver flashed in his eyes. "But I won't let you ignore it forever."

───────

AFTER SEVERAL BUSINESS MEETINGS, followed by a multitude of calls, Rillian finally went in search of Dayna. The suns were setting, sending a purple haze over Kor Magna.

In a few more hours, the Dark Nebula would be bursting at the seams—his restaurants full, his clubs pumping, and his gaming tables packed.

For Rillian, success at all costs wasn't just a desire, it was a primal need. When you came from nothing, worse than nothing, then all you dreamed about was holding the world in your palm.

He entered the gym, only to find it empty. But he spotted a towel, water bottle, and sweater left on a bench. Even from across the room, he scented Dayna on the fabric.

The penthouse floor of the Dark Nebula Casino was his own private domain—his office, bedroom, and gym. He'd never shared it with anyone before and had always hated people in his private space. Tannon, his head of security, had nearly had a fit when Rillian had brought

Dayna to the Dark Nebula. He'd called her and her new symbiont a risk.

Rillian picked up her sweater and pulled in a deep breath. Funny that he liked seeing Dayna's things around, or hearing her walk past his door, sensing the strong pulse of her energy in the air.

The whine of a laser weapon made him raise his head. His gaze moved to the adjoining doorway and he smiled.

Of course she'd be in his weapons room.

When he entered the windowless space, the scent of metal and smoke met his enhanced senses. The walls were lined with all kinds of weapons—from swords and staffs like those used by the gladiators in the arena to his collection of projectile and laser weapons.

Dayna stood in the center of the space, a laser pistol held with both hands, firing at an electronic target at the far end of the room. The program was a challenging one. The target moved and shifted, lights strobing to confuse her.

Her feet were apart, her body relaxed, her gaze narrowed with concentration. She twisted a little each time she fired, easy and controlled. He could easily see her training. He was well aware of her past job as a law enforcement officer on Earth. Rillian usually avoided law enforcement—a deep-seated habit from his childhood. But law enforcement on Carthago was rather ineffectual. On this wild desert world, people made their own rules. Besides, his wealth and power now meant they bowed to his every whim. He was a law unto himself.

Just how he liked it.

He continued to watch Dayna. She commanded attention. She was tall for a woman from Earth, and held herself in a way that said she was comfortable in her body and had full confidence in her abilities.

Yes, this human woman was...compelling. Long legs and thick, brown hair, with light brown eyes circled by a darker rim. A strong face and an even stronger will.

In his time, Rillian had seen physically stronger people than Dayna buckle under the burden of hosting a symbiont. She'd arrived here, half-dead and feverish. Her skin had been sallow and her hair lank. She'd lost weight during her captivity and ordeal with the desert witch.

But within days of coming to the Dark Nebula Casino, she'd pushed herself. She'd eaten, regained her strength, and gotten herself into his gym. She worked out every day, pushing herself to exhaustion. When she wasn't in the gym, she was in his casino, talking to people and familiarizing herself with life on Carthago.

What she wouldn't do was feed.

That was a challenge Dayna would have to face before too long.

Finally, the program finished and Dayna lowered her weapon.

"You only missed one target," Rillian said. "Impressive."

Her head whipped around. "I'll get it next time."

He strode closer, nodding at the weapon in her hand. "The EX-1020 is too large for you."

She shrugged a shoulder. "I'm trying them. They're not mine anyway." She set the weapon back onto the rack. "I kind of miss my Glock." She sighed. "And the cops I used to work with. A few of us used to meet weekly at the firing range."

Rillian leaned against the wall. "Yet you'd left your law enforcement job." He knew she'd been on a transport headed to join the security team at Fortuna Space Station when she'd been abducted.

Her mouth tightened. "I needed a change."

He detected a story, but he didn't push her. Right now, he felt the need to put a smile on her face, not a frown. "Come with me."

She shot him a suspicious look.

"I promise I don't have anything nefarious planned. I had Tannon copy all the data on the search for Zaabha. I have it ready for you."

Her eyes lit. "Excellent. I want to see the map that Neve and Corsair recovered from the desert witch."

Neve Haynes, another Earth woman, and her lover, the caravan master Corsair, had rescued Dayna from the witch on a hunt for a map to Zaabha. Neve was determined to find the desert arena because Ever Haynes was her sister.

When he strode into his office, Dayna was right behind him. He waved her toward an adjoining door. "I had Tannon set you up in the conference room off my office."

"Bet he loved that."

She stepped inside and pulled up short. A brand-new comp rested on the table, along with several files. The windows in this room weren't floor-to-ceiling, but the long bank of glass still afforded a good view of the city. Rillian liked looking out on Kor Magna from high above. He'd seen the backstreets up close and personal as a child, he had no desire to get too close to them again.

For a second, he remembered the other hardened, tough people he'd run with before he'd clawed his way out and made his fortune. People he'd once called friends. He shook his head. The past was always best left in the past.

"This is great, Rillian." Dayna picked up a stack of images off the table. "Thank you."

He'd given lovers rare flowers and expensive trinkets...but none of them had looked at him how Dayna looked at him now.

"Aerial images of the desert." She fanned them across the glossy table. "Is there a copy of the map that was inscribed on the rock?"

"Yes. On the comp and—" He touched the screen.

Light projected into the air around them. Dayna's mouth opened, and she twirled through the map projection. "Amazing."

Rillian took in the display of the map symbols and text. "Unfortunately, no one has been able to make sense of it yet."

Her mouth tightened. "Not even Zhim and Ryan?"

He shook his head. Even Carthago's premier information merchant and his human lover hadn't been able to decode it. "I have a team working day and night on it."

Dayna's shoulders slumped.

Rillian wanted to touch her, needed to touch her. Instead, he curled his fingers into his palm. "We *will* decode it."

"I want Ever and Sam safe." Determination filled her tone.

"We won't stop until we find them."

She made a shooing motion with her hand. "Now go. I'm sure you have gazillions to make and I want to get to work."

"Gazillions?"

Her lips twitched. "Obscene amounts of money."

He arched a brow. "Why bother making small amounts of money?"

She shook her head, shooing him again.

"I think you're forgetting whose casino this is," he said.

She smiled at him. "No. I just think you are far too used to bowing and scraping from all your minions. I just want to mix things up for you a bit."

With a shake of his head and a reluctant smile, Rillian headed for the door. "I've arranged for the kitchen to deliver you some dinner shortly."

A gusty sigh. "You're always feeding me."

"I like looking after you, Dayna." He saw surprise widen her eyes before he slipped out of the door. "Don't stay up too late."

"Yes, mom," she called back.

CHAPTER TWO

She woke in darkness, hearing a startled, terrified noise. Then she realized that the sound had come from her own throat.

Dayna's heartbeat pounded loudly in her ears. She shoved the sheets off her body and glanced at the fancy timepiece beside the bed.

She'd only been asleep for thirty minutes before the nightmares had come. A sob caught in her throat. For months, she'd only managed to sleep in tiny fits and bursts. She kept waiting for it to get better.

She scrambled across the bed, with none of her normal control or athleticism. With an awkward tumble, she half fell off the bed and the soft, plush carpet broke her fall. She stared blindly at the big, opulent bed drenched in night shadows.

In her head, all she could see was rough walls and hear pained screams. She imagined the faces of Ever and Sam. Still captives. Pain stabbed through Dayna's belly and she doubled over with a cry. The images fled, and all she could feel was an intense hunger that threatened to consume her.

Panic had her skidding backward across the floor until she bumped into the wall. She panted, trying to find some control. She'd always prided herself on her control, on being level-headed.

Now, she felt like she was choking. She felt the foreign presence inside her—quiet, still, but hungry.

Dayna swallowed a sob. All her life, she'd been practical, sensible, and take-charge. Only once she hadn't been, and her pretty, young sister had paid the price. Old, time-worn memories joined her more recent ones.

And in her chest, she felt something move.

Oh, God. She needed to get out.

Leaping to her feet, she raced for the door and slammed it open.

A guard dressed in a uniform of unrelieved black stood at her door. When he saw her, he straightened, his eyes widening.

Dayna didn't pause. She ran into the hall and bumped into him. Forgetting her newfound strength, she sent him flying.

She didn't stop, hurtling down the hallway, her bare feet slapping on the slick floor. The sheet of glass on one side of the corridor revealed the bright lights of the city below. Several enormous towers of glass and light speared into the night sky. And hanging in the dark sky above were two huge moons.

Hunger shifted inside her and her vision blurred. She wanted. She *needed*. With a sob, she spun and ran again.

Sound, light, and sensation crashed in on her, and the chaotic mess made her stumble. She slammed into the sleek double doors at the end of the hall and they flew open.

She ran into Rillian's office and almost crashed to the floor. As air sawed in and out of her lungs, her gaze moved over the room. The lights were dim, the only illumination coming from a wall covered in several clear, thin screens. They all showed live feed from the busy casino below. The black desk in front of the windows was empty.

Her gaze went to the screens and the people on them. So many people. She swallowed, pushing at her tangled hair. So many heartbeats. Even from here, on the highest penthouse level of the building, she felt the throb of energy coming out from the mass below.

She was a danger to all of them.

"Dayna."

The deep, masculine drawl made goose bumps break out on her skin.

She turned her head slowly and spotted him sitting in a chair in the dark. With her newly enhanced vision, she could easily make out his silhouette. He still wore the white shirt from earlier, and it shone in the darkness while his face remained hidden by the shadows.

"Bad night?" he asked.

She took a step toward him. She hated that tone—so smooth and unruffled. So controlled, when she was out of control.

He reached out and set a glass down on the side table beside his chair. The only sound in the room was the tinkle of ice. Even from across the office, she could smell the alcohol. The alien inside her gave her increased strength and enhanced senses that she'd never had as a human.

Rillian rose in a single, elegant move.

He took one step toward her, and suddenly Dayna was aware that she wasn't the biggest predator in the room.

"I hate this," she bit out. "I hate being out of control. I hate not being myself."

"Your symbiont is hungry. You need to feed."

"No." Her stomach churned.

"You can't ignore it."

The command in his voice made her anger spike. Something twisted inside her. The pain grew in her chest and hunger exploded. She made a choked sound and everything that she'd been fighting to hold back unleashed.

All rational thought gone, Dayna rushed at Rillian.

HE CAUGHT her as she flew at him.

The symbiont living inside Dayna made her strong... but Rillian's was stronger.

He held her as she snarled and struggled. He wrapped his arms around her, pulling her up against his chest, making sure she didn't hurt herself.

He'd been expecting this. She'd worked hard to get healthier, but she kept ignoring the major change to her body.

She shoved at him and he used more strength to hold her. A fighter, this one. He'd known all manner of women during his life, but this one defied logic. The symbiont should have killed her, but instead she'd survived. Still, instead of accepting it, she continued to fight.

She fascinated him.

He tried not to notice how her sleep shirt rode up, baring long, smooth legs. Rillian clamped down on his body's response. She was in his care. He let her struggle and fight against him until finally she sagged, exhausted.

"Dayna—"

"Don't say it."

"Being silent won't change things. You need to feed."

She tipped that strong, interesting face up to his, and gold flashed through her eyes. "*No.*"

"I've energy to spare," he told her. "Take it. It will help you control it."

She jerked away from him, stumbling back. "I'm not a leech."

Spinning, she faced the windows and wrapped her arms around herself. She stared through the glass, but he knew she wasn't looking at the view. Her chin dropped to her chest.

"Dayna, in the two weeks you've been here, you've been adjusting well. You suffered a terrible ordeal—"

Her head jerked up and she looked at him over her shoulder. "I can handle it. I was a cop. I've been through tough situations before."

"You don't have to handle it alone," he said.

She spun. "Did you? When you got your symbiont? Did you get help and lean on someone?"

His jaw clenched. No, he'd writhed in agony alone in the darkness. "This isn't about me."

She turned away. "I just want..."

He waited for her to finish, but she didn't say anything else. He took a step closer, watching her reflection in the window.

"You want things to be as they were before? To be the same woman you were before? Going back isn't an option, Dayna."

"I know that." She gave a harsh laugh. "I learned that lesson as a little girl."

Again, Rillian felt the strange and unfamiliar need to ease this woman's hurts. He fought not to shift restlessly.

She pushed a hand through her hair. "God, I hate that you always see me at my worst."

"Funny, I always think how strong, competent, and courageous you appear."

She turned, her gaze on his face. Those eyes reminded him of polished stones from the moon of Anarlia, and were so direct, he found himself feeling strangely exposed.

"I've been planning an exhibition fight with Galen—the House of Galen against the House of Rone. It's in two days' time. You'll get to see your friends."

A flash of panic appeared in her eyes before she looked away. "I don't want to go."

"Dayna—"

"I...I don't want to hurt them."

Of course, her first thought was for others. "You won't."

"You don't know that!" Her voice rose. "You don't know how I feel sometimes. So hungry, so on edge."

He met her gaze in the window. "I know."

Her body shuddered. "I feel like the leash is slipping."

"Because you need to feed."

"No!" But then her eyes flashed gold and she moved fast, spinning and leaping on him.

Her speed took him by surprise and she managed to take him down. They crashed to the floor and her legs straddled his hips. She gripped his wrists and slammed them to the floor above his head.

Dayna's eyes were shifting, brown turning to molten gold. Her symbiont was fighting for control.

Rillian thrust his body upward and they rolled across the floor of his office. She snarled and pushed to get on top again. They strained against each other. Drak, she was stronger than he'd thought.

They rolled again, legs thrashing. They smashed into a cabinet and it toppled beside them, glass shattering.

Suddenly, the doors flew open and his security guards rushed in, laser weapons raised.

"Stay back," Rillian roared at them. "Get out."

Dayna made a pained, animalistic noise and went for his throat. This time, he rolled, and pinned her beneath him.

"Do you want your friends to see you like this?" he asked harshly.

She bucked up against him.

He held her down and tore his shirt open. Fastenings bounced across the floor. Her gaze flickered, sliding down his body. He grabbed one of her hands and pressed her palm against his skin.

"Feed."

She let out a sob and shook her head wildly.

He watched, with stunned admiration, as she fought for control. She gulped in large breaths and he watched the gold slowly bleed from her eyes.

Her fingers flexed on his chest and now he felt a rush of desire. His cock hardened, like he was a drakking untried teen, not a man in full control of his body.

Oh, he wanted Dayna. Wanted her spread out beneath him, naked and taking him. But he had vowed to help her, not take advantage of her. He'd promised Galen.

Rillian shifted, pulling them both up to sit. She didn't need to feel his cock digging into her belly. She sat there, still a bit dazed, and fighting to pull herself back together.

"Thank you." Her words were stiff.

"You will need to feed your symbiont eventually, Dayna. You know I'm here to help you."

She hunched her shoulders. "We both know you're my prison guard." There was acid in her voice.

"Your guardian." Rillian would never allow himself to take advantage of a woman at her most vulnerable, and he would never allow himself to lose control. He would take care of her, no matter what. Studying her face, he saw how tired she looked. Dark smudges underscored her eyes. "Are you sleeping?"

Her lips pressed together. "I...I have nightmares. Of the underground fight rings, of Zaabha, of the witch."

Brown eyes met his. "Of what could be happening to Ever and Sam."

"You need to rest. You can't help them if you're exhausted."

She shook her head. "And I can't rest knowing they aren't safe."

He reached out, his fingers pressing to her cheekbone. "You don't even know them."

"I know what it's like to worry about someone. To not know where they are, to wonder what they're going through, to wonder what you could have done differently." There was old pain buried in her voice.

She needed to rest. If she wouldn't willingly help herself, then he would have to ensure it. Fortunately, his symbiont granted him several abilities. He stroked her cheek and watched her eyelids flutter closed.

As she collapsed, Rillian swept her into his arms, checking her brain wave patterns. She'd sleep soundly for several hours. He rose and headed for her room.

I will protect you, Dayna Caplan. Even from yourself. He shifted her and her head fell against his shoulder. Her lashes were dark against her cheeks. *And especially from me.*

CHAPTER THREE

"We can't wait to see you at the arena fight."

Dayna smiled at her friends on the screen. She was sitting in her new office, after several hours spent pouring over all the information on Zaabha.

"Me, too," she told Mia and Winter. She mostly meant it. She wanted to see them. Desperately. They hadn't known each other before their abduction, but the three of them had forged strong bonds in the darkness and nothing could break that.

But last night's horrible episode left Dayna feeling shaky.

"You look great, Dayna," Winter said.

She focused on her friend. Dark hair framed Winter's face. She had one blue eye and one milky white. The Thraxians had experimented on the former doctor and left her blind, but thankfully, the House of Galen healers had restored some of her sight.

"I had a good night's sleep." Thanks to a sneaky,

bossy casino owner. The man had knocked her out and she'd had her first good night's sleep. Still, it didn't mean she liked his methods.

Winter nodded. "Essential for healing."

"Did you talk to your father?" Mia asked.

Dayna nodded. "A few days ago." She'd made the call using Zhim's fancy wormhole communication technology. "He was upset, but glad I'm alive." It had been an awkward, sad conversation. She and her father had never been close, but their relationship had been damaged long before the Thraxians had taken her. Dayna shook off the old sadness. "So, enough about boring old me, how's life for you guys being all loved up with alien gladiators?"

Blonde-haired Mia grinned. "Ah-mazing."

Winter's nose wrinkled. "Mia's man does everything he can to make her happy. Spoils her rotten."

Mia snorted. "And Nero doesn't do the same to you?"

"Nero has grumpy and overbearing down to an art. He likes to do things he thinks are in my best interest. Without asking me first."

Sounded like someone else Dayna knew.

"He loves you," Mia said. "And you're educating the barbarian gladiator on a few things."

Now Winter smiled, love in her eyes. "He does, and I sure am."

The women both looked over their shoulders. "Hey, we have to go," Mia said. "We'll see you at the fight. Nothing like watching half naked, muscled gladiators battling each other to make you feel better."

Dayna laughed. God, she was so thrilled these two women were safe and happy. "See you then."

But when the screen winked out, she sat back in her chair, worry niggling at her. She was stronger, fitter...but this thing inside her meant she didn't trust herself. She blew out a breath. She needed to get a handle on controlling it.

Eyeing the time, she realized the casino would be starting to get busy. She usually did a lap of the place, testing her ability to be in a crowd. Besides, the cop in her liked checking out Rillian's security. There were a few improvements she'd make if she owned the place.

She headed out of the conference room. Rillian was shut up in his office, no doubt wheeling and dealing. She'd heard him earlier chewing someone out with an icy, cutting voice. Dayna had almost felt sorry for the poor sucker. She made it to the elevators and stepped inside.

As the elevator descended, Dayna pulled in a deep breath. She ran her hands down her fitted, black trousers. The doors opened and she stiffened her spine.

You can do this.

She stepped out onto the main floor of the Dark Nebula Casino.

The rush of sounds and sensations hit her and she closed her eyes, breathing deeply. *One. Two. Three.*

She would control this *thing* inside her. She was no danger to the people here. Her two shadows stood behind her. Everywhere she went, two of Rillian's security guards appeared out of nowhere, as they always did when she left the penthouse.

She scanned the casino. Black walls were accented by huge vases of flowers in purple and red. The alien gaming tables were all red as well, and packed with people. She looked up, wonder making her chest tighten. Didn't matter how many times she saw it, it was still the most beautiful thing she'd seen. The ceiling was covered in twinkling stars and the gorgeous hues of a multicolored nebula. It looked so real.

The place was all glitz and class. It was filled to the brim with people...or rather, aliens. She glanced at a tall woman, over six feet, who was wearing a stunning silver dress, with space for a tail that flicked back and forth behind her. Not far away, a tall red-skinned alien was laughing as he threw something on a table. He made her think of the biblical demons from her Sunday-school classes. She turned and came face-to-face with another alien male. He towered over her and sported a set of horns that made her gut tighten. His skin was pearly white, but he still reminded her far too much of the dark, horned Thraxians.

Her throat tightened, memories rising up like dark bubbles. Turning away, her gaze fell on a neatly hidden camera. The place was riddled with them and she'd spent several hours mapping them all out. She imagined Rillian up in his office, watching those screens. Nothing went on in his domain without him knowing.

All too easily, she recalled that chaotic, wild moment in his office the night before. Their fight, the blood pumping through her veins, the energy pumping off him. When he pressed her palm to his warm skin...

She shifted, pressing her thighs together. She was acutely aware that her panties were wet.

Dayna closed her eyes. Rillian's handsome face filled her mind. When she'd been rolling around on the floor with him, she hadn't missed the hard bulge in his trousers.

She crossed her arms. It had probably just been a reaction to the heightened emotions. She straightened her shoulders, determined to put it out of her mind. The last thing she needed in her out-of-control life was a man.

She strode into the casino, steeling herself against the onslaught of sensation.

If she narrowed her eyes, she could almost imagine she was back on Earth. She'd taken a trip to Atlantic City once with some friends from the forensics lab. She'd hated the tired, worn casino they'd stayed at. It had been so seedy. There was absolutely nothing tired or worn or seedy about the Dark Nebula.

Dayna did a lap of the floor, looking at the different games on offer. People were flashing medallion-like coins, which she knew acted as a sort of credit card on Carthago. Others were piling coins up on the tables. She shook her head. She couldn't understand tossing good money away for the spin of a wheel, the roll of the dice, or the...she wasn't even sure what the dealer was throwing.

"Dayna," a bright, cheery voice called out.

She turned and saw one of the casino cocktail waitresses standing nearby with an almost empty tray of drinks. The woman was gorgeous, with a long, sleek body sheathed in a black, slinky dress. Her green hair fell in a stunning wave to her waist.

"Briella. Hi." Dayna smiled.

"Taking your usual walk around?" the woman asked with a grin.

Dayna nodded. She'd spent a fair bit of time

meeting the casino staff and discreetly pumping them for information on Rillian. But the man ran a tight ship, and he had his staff's loyalty. None of them would talk, except to say he was a tough but fair boss.

"How are things?" Dayna asked.

Briella lifted a shoulder. "Great. Busy today and my feet are killing me." The woman tilted her head. "You look...rested."

Dayna made a face. She didn't want to think about her forced sleep. He didn't have the right to go around zapping people into unconsciousness. She was tired of having her choices taken away from her.

"Something like that. And now I'm hungry." The regular kind of hungry, thankfully.

Briella grinned. "Oh, I bet Chef Derol has saved something for you."

Dayna snorted. "He threatened to chop my fingers off if he caught me in his kitchen again."

The waitress laughed. "That grumpy, temperamental man doesn't let anyone in his part of the kitchen. Last time you were there, I saw him *smile* at you. He doesn't even smile for Rillian."

Thoughts of the barbs she regularly traded with the slim chef made Dayna smile. Chef Derol took temperamental to new levels.

"I've got to get a new load of drinks." Briella shifted her tray with practiced ease. "I'll see you later."

Dayna lifted a hand as the woman hurried off. She turned and headed in the direction of the kitchens. When she pushed through the large doors, she was assailed by the smell of cooking food and a bustle of frenetic activity.

She walked along the long benches, nodding at several chefs she'd met before. Most of the food on the benches, being mixed in bowls or cooked in pots, was unrecognizable. Her stomach did a slow turn. She'd discovered a lot of alien food did not agree with the human palate.

Spotting a bowl of tiny, bright-purple fruit, she snatched one up and took a bite. Mmm, *braxha* were tart and delicious.

"I don't tolerate thieves in my kitchen."

The grumpy, high-pitched voice made her spin and swallow a smile.

Chef Derol stood nearby, glaring at her. He held himself like the master of his domain, chin lifted. Despite his silver-gray skin, bald head, and long, painfully thin body, he wouldn't have been out of place in a posh French restaurant with his attitude.

"Derol, a pleasure to see you."

"*Chef* Derol, Dayna Caplan."

She smiled. "Having a good day?"

"I have several hundred mouths to feed, most who will mindlessly shove my creations in their mouths as they gamble." He held up an imperious hand. "They will not appreciate the skill, the talent, and the mastery of the delicacies that they are eating."

"You're such a humble guy, Chef. It was the first thing I noticed about you."

His eyes narrowed. "And you are a respectful,

reserved woman. It was the first thing I noticed about you."

She almost laughed. She wasn't sure how this daily exchange of barbs had started, but it was one of the highlights of her existence right now. "Ooh, good one." She leaned against one of the benches. "How long have you been saving that one?"

"A few days." He snatched the fruit from her hand.

"Hey!"

"That *braxha* isn't ripe." He sniffed and handed over a larger green fruit that had been partially hollowed out and filled with...something yellow. "Try this."

When in Rome. She prayed the man wasn't trying to poison her. She took a bite and her eyes widened. She chewed and swallowed. Oh, God, it was the most delicious thing she'd ever eaten. Derol was watching her expectantly.

She took another bite. "It's okay."

Derol's eyes narrowed and his lips twitched. She was pretty sure the man was trying not to laugh. "You are an unrefined pain."

"I love you, too."

"Rillian requested I make it for you."

Oh? She took another bite of the luscious fruit, her mind once again turning to the man she couldn't seem to stop thinking about.

Suddenly, the chef looked past her and straightened. She heard the chatter in the kitchen decrease. She sensed him coming, so didn't need to look.

"Rillian." Derol sketched a small bow.

Dayna fought not to roll her eyes, and took another bite of the deliciousness in her hand.

A female chef stepped forward. "What can we get for you, sir?"

Rillian held up a hand. "I'm fine, thank you." His silver-threaded gaze landed on Dayna. "I'm here for Dayna."

Damn her stupid heart for going pitty-pat in her chest. That was one stupid reaction she was happy to blame on her symbiont.

RILLIAN LED Dayna out of the kitchen, watching several chefs wave goodbye. He frowned. He was pretty sure Chef Derol was smiling. Derol might be the best chef on all of Carthago, but the man never smiled.

Dayna had that effect on people. When people talked, she listened. They liked talking with her.

He'd just stepped through the door when a young server grabbed Dayna's arm.

"Hi, Dayna. Wanted to thank you for that advice you gave me."

Rillian scowled at the enthusiastic young man holding Dayna's arm and grinning at her.

"Robi. How did it go?" Dayna smiled back.

"It was *amazing*. I did everything you suggested—" The young man stepped closer and spotted Rillian.

The man's face froze. He swallowed slowly. "Uh, sorry to interrupt, sir."

Rillian's gaze fell to the man's hand. Robi took the hint, releasing Dayna and stepping back.

"I...uh, I have...things." Robi waved a nervous hand in the air.

"Don't mind him," Dayna said. "Did she say yes?"

Robi didn't take his eyes off Rillian. "Who?"

"Your girlfriend. When you told her you were in love with her?"

Robi's attention finally turned back to Dayna. His face was glowing. "Yes. She loved the flowers and the meal. She's moving in." A wary glance at Rillian. "I'd better get back to work."

Dayna fell into step beside Rillian as they continued on their way.

"Do you make friends with everyone?" he asked.

"Do you intimidate everyone?"

"Not you." He bypassed the main casino area, heading for a bank of private staff elevators. The shiny metal doors opened and he waved her inside.

She leaned against the wall and crossed her arms. "I'm not easily intimidated."

They moved upward. "So I've learned."

"And I'm still pissed at you."

"I sensed that." He leaned over, watching as she went still. He might not intimidate her, but she noticed him. He swiped his thumb beside her lips.

"What are you doing?" Her voice had lowered.

"You have some *Tnarrian* cream there." He wiped it off her skin, wondering for about the hundredth time what she tasted like. His gaze locked with hers, he lifted his thumb to his mouth and sucked it clean.

He tasted her through the rich flavor, a hint of something bold and spicy. "Intimidated?"

She cleared her throat. "You'll have to do better than that. Where are we going?"

Fascinating, tempting woman. He straightened. "Back to the penthouse." He didn't want to admit that he'd seen her on his screens and had felt the sudden urge for her company. "I didn't want you to overdo it."

She spun, her eyes glinting. "I decide how I'm feeling, Rillian, not you. I've been an adult a very long time." She poked him in the chest. "And you do not go around zapping me to sleep."

"You needed the rest."

"I know that, but it's my choice, not yours to take from me. I've had the Thraxians and then that fucking desert witch take all my choices away, I won't let you do it too."

Rillian froze. "You're comparing my wanting to look after you to them?"

She sighed. "I know you mean well—"

"I promised Galen I'd take care of you."

Her lips flattened. "I know you took me on as a favor to him." She looked at the wall.

Rillian gripped her chin and forced her gaze to his. "That might be how it started, but I feel a very strong need to see to your wellbeing."

The air in the elevator turned charged.

Then he felt something inside him stir, something else with primal, vicious needs. He let her go and stepped back abruptly. Something about Dayna Caplan stirred up things best left dormant.

The elevator slowed. "How's your work on the search for Zaabha going?"

"Not good." They exited the elevator. "The map appears useless and so far, there are no solid leads to where Zaabha is."

He watched her fingers flex. "Give it time."

She burst into the office. "Ever and Sam haven't got time, Rillian. You know the Thraxians and what they're capable of." She thrust her hands into her hair. "God, those poor women might not even be alive."

He felt the emotions pumping off her. Far too strong to be sympathy for two strangers. "This is more than a human looking out for a fellow human."

"I was a homicide detective. It was my job to—"

"It's more than just a job driving you."

She spun to face him. "My sister was kidnapped when she was five and I was eight. Right out of our front yard." The words burst out of her.

"I'm sorry."

"My parents..." she shook her head. "It was the worst time in the world. We had no idea where she was, or what was happening to her." Her voice hitched. "I know what it is to pray, wonder, hope, despair, and drown in the pain when someone is missing."

And then she'd been through that nightmare herself. "Did you get her back?"

Dayna's gaze met his, and it was filled with pain and sorrow. "Her body was found a week later." She dropped the printed images, the light from the projection playing over her face. "She'd been tortured and killed."

35

Rillian had seen terrible things, but the death of a child was always the worst. "I'm very sorry."

A muscle ticked in Dayna's jaw. "I was supposed to be watching her."

"Dayna—"

She shook her head. "My parents fell apart and that day, I decided I would help stop other monsters who took the lives of the innocent." Suddenly a grimace crossed her face. She pressed a hand to her chest.

"What's wrong?"

She made a choked noise, panic in her eyes. *Drak.* Her emotions had stirred up her hungry symbiont. "You need to feed." He stepped closer.

She held out a hand. "No."

"You're being stubborn."

"I'm not an animal or a damn vampire. I *will* control this." Lines bracketed her mouth.

"The longer you starve your symbiont, the more dangerous it gets."

She gritted her teeth and he saw misery in her eyes.

"I won't let you lose control." He took another step toward her.

There was a knock at the door and Rillian bit back his frustration. He'd told his assistant to only interrupt him if it was vitally important. Dayna turned away from him.

He let out a harsh breath. "Come in."

Tannon Gi stepped inside. Rillian's head of security had brown hair cut short, a rugged face, and colorless eyes that sparkled brightly, like Friskan diamonds. The man looked like he should be out on a battlefield somewhere.

"Rillian, there's been a disturbance in the casino."

"Can't you handle it?" Rillian knew Tannon wouldn't miss the tension in the room.

"No. You need to see this."

The man's tone made Rillian straighten. He saw Dayna do the same thing. If there was one thing Tannon wasn't known for, it was exaggeration.

"What's happened?" Dayna asked.

"Someone's been murdered," Tannon answered. "On the main casino floor."

CHAPTER FOUR

W hen Rillian, Tannon, and several security guards stepped into the glass-encased elevator, Dayna followed. She shot Rillian a look, daring him to stop her.

He just lifted one dark brow, and that elegant, controlled move made her want to mess him up. To get a reaction.

Control, Dayna. As the fancy elevator zoomed downward, she rubbed the stone between her breasts. The hunger was still there, banked for now. Not for the first time, she wondered what feeding off Rillian would feel like.

She'd been so close to feeding off him the night before. She stared at the back of his head. His hard body had been pressed against hers, all that lethal strength and the pulse of power. Desire curled hot and hard in her belly.

The elevator opened and the mass of noise hit her. They stepped out onto the main floor of the casino.

Yep, it didn't matter how many times she walked the casino floor, the sensory overload packed a punch. Just like its owner.

Rillian strode at the front of their small group. The crowd parted for him with ease. He sure caused a stir. Nearly every head turned to watch him—men with envy, and women with...well, most of them were watching him for a very different reason. The desire she saw made her stomach sour.

A singer was up on a nearby stage. She was long and lean, and dressed in a slick, red catsuit that looked painted onto her body. Her dark, curly hair was piled up in a complicated design. Her voice was a high warble, and the music sounded discordant to Dayna's ears, but many in the crowd were watching with rapt expressions. The woman's hungry gaze followed Rillian across the room.

Get in line, lady. What, did every woman on Carthago fall at the man's feet?

They moved toward a gaming table in the center of the room. It was comprised of two sections, with a narrow bit in the middle, and a blood-red top. Unlike the other tables in the room, however, there were no eager players standing by it. It had been cordoned off by the security guards.

And draped backward on one chair was a woman in a bright-blue dress.

Dayna didn't need her former detective skills to know that the woman was dead.

"No one saw anything?" Rillian asked.

Tannon shook his head.

"Security footage?" Dayna asked.

The big man glanced at her and she wondered if he ever smiled. "We're analyzing it now."

Dayna took in the victim. Most of her face was covered by pale-blonde hair. From what Dayna could see, her features were beautifully made-up, and the victim had faint scales on her blue-tinted skin.

But Dayna made herself look past the makeup and the long, blue dress. She stepped closer, and saw one of the woman's hands dangling down by her side. As the others talked, Rillian barking out questions, Dayna crouched.

The woman had callused hands. Her nails were quite short, even though they were painted fire-engine red. For a moment, Dayna felt like she was back on the force. This felt familiar and she felt in control. She didn't feel like that wild, scared woman she'd been last night.

She grabbed a pen from her pocket and touched the woman's fancy, heeled shoe. They were strapped to her ankles, but when Dayna pushed the shoe down, she could see that the material had left raw, red marks on the woman's foot. They were new. She wasn't used to wearing them.

"Dayna?" Rillian's voice came from close behind her.

"Sorry." She stood. "Force of habit." She shoved her hands in the pockets of her trousers.

He studied her steadily. "Come with me to the security room. We can watch the camera footage."

Excitement winged through her. She nodded, glad to

be involved. She followed the small group out of the main casino.

The second trip in the elevator was much shorter. When they stepped out into the high-tech security room, she gasped. There were screens everywhere, and more black-uniformed security members sitting at computers. In the center of the room was a holographic projection of the entire casino. It was covered in a scramble of red, orange, blue and green dots and lines. Damn, she wanted to know what they all represented.

She wasn't too proud to admit she was a little bit turned on.

Rillian stopped beside her, his shoulder brushing hers. "I've seen women look at the rarest jewels the same way you're looking at my security room right now." His voice was ripe with amusement.

"I'm not impressed by jewelry."

He was silent for a beat. "I'm not surprised."

Someone pushed out chairs for them at a comp screen, but neither of them sat. They stood and watched the footage replay on a screen. The woman had arrived, flanked by two big men. She moved over to the table, placing her bet. The camera angles weren't great and there wasn't a good view of her face. Then, Dayna watched as one of the men moved, and their view of the woman was completely blocked. Then both men stepped away and left. The woman was slumped in her chair, looking like she was resting.

"Nothing unusual, sir," one of the security team said. "Maybe her lovers wanted to get rid of her?"

Dayna cleared her throat. "The man on her right

purposely blocked the camera. The other did something to her, you can just see his arm move, and whatever it was presumably killed her."

Everyone in the room turned to look at Dayna. But she'd worked NYPD for over ten years and survived the Thraxians. It would take more than an alien security team to rattle her.

"Neither man gave us a clear view of their faces. They knew where your cameras were."

Rillian's dark gaze narrowed, silver sparking in his eyes like lightning. "Go on."

"She's not a glitzy party girl. She's got calluses on her hands, and it didn't look like she was used to wearing the fancy shoes she had on. And she didn't seem particularly happy coming in with them."

A female security team member cleared her throat. "She came willingly. She didn't look scared."

Dayna nodded. "Yes, but you never get a full view of her face. However, if you look, you'll see her shoulders are tense, her hand is clenched in a fist."

"She was under stress." Rillian glanced back at the screen. "Tannon, keep analyzing the footage and inform me on the results of the autopsy. I want to know who she was, and why she was killed in my casino in such a deliberate fashion."

Dayna straightened. "I'd like to help."

Those silver eyes met hers. "Okay."

She relaxed. "Thank you."

"Your observation skills are impressive."

That faint praise made her want to flush. "It used to be my job."

"Sir?" a female security member called out. "Facial recognition came back with the match. The victim was a casino waitress here at the Dark Nebula. She's listed as a single mother who started work here about two months ago."

Dayna's stomach sank. The woman had been a mother?

"Dayna was correct." Tannon tapped on a screen. "Yana Dray wasn't a party girl or mistress. She was a waitress at the Dark Star restaurant here in the casino."

God. For a second, Dayna was eight years old again, watching the big detective with the balding head and tired eyes telling her and her parents that Gwendolyn was dead. Some child was out there, about to get the same news.

A muscle ticked in Rillian's jaw. "She was one of ours."

Everyone in the security room went quiet.

"Wait." Tannon tapped again. "A message from the team removing the body. They found a note beneath her."

"A note?" Dayna stepped forward, and watched as an image flashed up on the screen.

It was covered in alien text Dayna couldn't read. She had an implant that allowed her to speak and understand various languages, but she couldn't read them.

"What does it say?" she asked.

Rillian's mouth turned into a flat line. "This is just the beginning. Abandon the House of Galen, or more will die."

RILLIAN SAT IN HIS OFFICE, with the imperator of the House of Galen on his comp screen. He'd just finished outlining the situation for Galen.

"Drak." Galen's scarred face was unhappy. His right eye—the one not covered by a black eyepatch—was cold.

"This has to be the Thraxians. We need to find Zaabha, Galen, and shut it down once and for all. The Thraxians and the Srinar have overstepped too many boundaries."

The Srinar, a plague-ridden species who liked operating in the darkest spaces of Carthago, were allies of the Thraxians. They had to be shown a lesson as well.

"Agreed," Galen said. "I have Zhim and Ryan working on the map that Neve and Corsair recovered. It's not going well. They tell me that part of the map is missing. They need some sort of key to unlock it and we have no idea what or where that might be."

Rillian sat back in his chair. "At the witch's lair?"

"We searched it from top to bottom. We didn't find anything." A muscle ticked in Galen's jaw. "There's more. The House of Thrax has gone into complete lockdown. They aren't accepting fights, not seeing anybody, not even taking in more gladiators. My guess is that they are pulling back to protect Zaabha."

"It's too late for that," Rillian said darkly. "Especially when they're leaving dead bodies in my casino." He felt his anger spike and forced it down. "Killing my people."

"The Thraxians don't understand subtleties. They probably believed it would get you to back off."

"They don't know me very well, then."

"And I have two women I intend to rescue from Zaabha." The imperator's voice was unyielding. "I won't stop until Ever Haynes and Sam Santos are free."

"You have my support."

Galen inclined his head, then his single, ice-blue eye narrowed. "How's Dayna?"

"She's a fighter. She'll make it, but she's...stubborn."

Galen almost smiled. "That seems to be a common trait for the women of Earth." The man's voice was dry.

Rillian steepled his hands together. "You'd know. Everyone's talking about the infamous Galen going soft for damsels in need of rescue."

The imperator snorted. "With my gladiators falling in love with Earth women every time they step into the arena, I hardly have a choice."

"Keep your eyes open, Galen. If the Thraxians are warning me off helping you, that means they're coming for you."

Galen's gaze narrowed. "I'll be waiting. See you at the exhibition match tomorrow."

Rillian nodded. "Dayna is apprehensive, but excited."

"The women, especially Winter and Mia, are eager to see her."

After ending the call, Rillian checked in with Tannon, only to discover that there were no updates on Yana Dray's murder. Frustrated, he wandered toward the conference room.

Dayna sat hunched over her comp screen, tapping away. It was nice to hear her working so close to his office. He shook his head. He'd always valued his space, but for some reason he liked this woman here. He knocked on the door and when she called out a distracted hello, he walked closer.

She had papers spread over the table and a frown creased her brow.

"Dayna?"

She looked up at him and blinked. "Yes?"

He moved closer. "What are you doing?"

"Going over Yana's murder."

"How long have you been working?" he asked.

Her frown deepened, and she tilted her neck to stretch it. "What time is it?"

"Late."

"Shit. A while. I lost track of time." She set the comp down. "Not the first time I've gotten lost in a case."

"Have you eaten anything?"

She shook her head.

He pulled out his sleek personal communicator and ordered some food. When he looked back, she was tapping on the comp again. "Have you found anything?"

"I did find an image of one of the men from a better angle from a secondary camera. I sent it to Tannon."

Rillian walked closer, glancing out the window at the lovely view of the flat-topped Raddos Mountains in the distance. "I know who murdered her."

Dayna's head shot up. "You do?"

"This is a message from the Thraxians. They don't want Zaabha found."

Her face hardened. "I figured as much. That arena needs to be shut down. I wasn't there long, but...it was horrible. The chanting spectators who wanted blood.

The terrible cells. I never got to see the champion of Zaabha, but they shouted and screamed for her." Dayna shook her head, looking like she wanted to shake the memories away.

"Are you still having nightmares?"

She brushed her hair back. "Something tells me I'll have nightmares for the rest of my life." She lifted her chin. "But that's not what's important. Sam and Ever need to be rescued. Yana's family needs closure."

Rillian studied the stubborn line of her jaw. He wondered about her previous job solving murders. Did they still haunt her too? "It must have been difficult to tell people their loved ones were gone."

"Worst part of the job."

"And you'd been on the other side, too."

She nodded. "Hearing about Gwendolyn was horrible. It shattered our family. My parents were never the same and my mother died two years later. It's what spurred me to want to be a detective."

"But you were planning to leave it behind."

She leaned back, emotion churning in her eyes. "I was burned out. Other people's grief, the crimes I couldn't solve, the victims I failed... I decided to go into security. I decided I wanted to stop crimes *before* they happened."

A woman who gave her all to other people. She was damned admirable.

"And I want to find Ever and Sam more than anything," she added quietly.

"We'll find them." He sat on the table beside her, his tone lowering. "And we will *obliterate* Zaabha."

She stared at him. Rillian knew that particular tone had made many an opponent shudder in fear, but Dayna just looked curious.

"I believe you. Wow, I guess I don't ever want to piss you off."

"No, you don't."

She smiled at him, and Rillian wondered how long it had been since he'd spent time with a woman who didn't preen and work to impress him every second. His female companions were attracted to him, but they still feared him.

Attraction stirred in his blood and he quickly squelched it. But he'd never met anyone like Dayna Caplan.

There was a knock at the door. Rillian answered and waved the server in to set the food down on the table.

Dayna looked skeptically at the tray.

"Eat," he ordered.

She rolled her eyes, but plucked up an *aggla* berry. She tucked her legs beneath her on the chair.

"How is your symbiont today?" he asked.

She made a face, the light in her eyes dimming. "I try not to think about it."

"It's a part of you, now."

"I don't want it to be!" The words burst out of her. "It was forced on me."

"Mine was, too." He froze, mentally cursing himself. He'd never spoken about how he'd received his symbiont with anyone.

She looked up. "When?"

"When I was eighteen."

She gasped. "So young."

He shot her a small smile. "By the time I was eighteen, I hadn't been a child for a very long time." He flexed his hands, memories rising to the surface.

"How...did it happen?" she asked.

Usually, unwanted questions from anybody were swiftly shut down. There were things Rillian didn't want to share, and it paid to never give your enemies, opponents, and rivals anything that could be used as a weakness. But strangely, he found himself wanting to reveal some of his secrets.

"I grew up in the back streets of Kor Magna. My mother—not that she deserved or wanted that title—was a smuggler and a master thief."

Dayna sucked in a breath.

Unfamiliar emotions bit at Rillian. Drak, he'd buried his past way down deep a long time ago. Why was he dredging it up and telling it to Dayna?

"Go on," she said softly.

He drew in a deep breath. "I was following in her footsteps, and making a name for myself as a smuggler. And I was a successful one, until I stepped on the wrong toes. My symbiont was punishment from a rival."

Dayna's eyes went wide.

"I wasn't supposed to survive. But instead of dying like he had planned, I lived. And then I embraced my symbiont to make myself more powerful and successful." He rose. "You should, too."

"I...don't know if I can."

The emotion in her voice made Rillian's fingers curl into his palms. He wanted to touch her, but he forced his hands to stay by his sides. "From what I've seen so far, you are a frighteningly capable woman, Dayna."

"So I need to learn to...feed?"

"Yes. Most alien symbionts simply want to coexist happily with their host. If you can learn some give and take, you'll feel much better."

She tilted her head. "Is that what you do with your symbiont?"

No. Rillian pulled in a breath. He ruthlessly controlled his symbiont. It was one that could never truly be let loose.

"This isn't about me."

Her gaze narrowed. "You feed your symbiont."

"When required."

Those probing eyes didn't leave his face. Drak, Rillian felt like someone she'd arrested for a crime. He was certain she'd been very good at her job.

"Your symbiont requires more than just feeding."

"Enough, Dayna."

"No. You're asking me to accept this thing inside me, and do something that freaks me out." She pointed at her chest. "I hate the idea of risking someone's life by feeding from them. But you're giving me half-truths. I get the feeling you *don't* give your symbiont what it needs."

Rillian gritted his teeth. He'd spent a lifetime building his strength and power. Hiding the things he didn't want to show the world. "My life is none of your business and never will be."

Her head jerked like he'd hit her. "Right. The cool, controlled Rillian won't ever let anyone past his masks and shields. You spend your days handling me and everyone else in your damn little empire, but you never let your guard down enough to let anyone close."

"I don't want anyone close."

Her lips pressed together. "Got it. Loud and clear." She turned back to her computer.

Rillian stared at her downturned head, then swiveled and strode out.

CHAPTER FIVE

D ayna stepped out of the tunnel and into the stands of the Kor Magna Arena.

She took a second to take it all in. The huge oval of sand in the center, the rings of seating, and the flags fluttering off the towers in the evening breeze. The arena was made of a cream-colored stone that felt old. She could almost hear the sounds of ancient fights and screaming fans echoing around her.

"It's been here hundreds of years."

Rillian's deep voice made her turn her head. He stood beside her, clothed in a black suit that made him look equally handsome and dangerous.

They only stood inches apart, but it felt like a chasm. He'd avoided her all day and she'd worked in her office, getting more and more frustrated about every damn thing.

Somehow, he'd hurt her. She was stupid. One look and she knew he was a man who controlled every aspect of his life. She'd just fallen into such an easy routine with him, and felt...more than she should.

"But of course," he added, "over that time, it's evolved. The vicious fights to the death of old have given way to the displays of fighting skills and prowess we see today."

Dayna swallowed. Zaabha still had fights to the death. Bloody spectacles of pain and dying.

Rillian took her arm and instantly, she felt an electric zing.

Goddammit. The man was just too potent. He turned his head and their gazes met. For a second, it felt like the world stopped.

"Dayna...I'm sorry about last night."

"You don't need to apologize."

"I don't let people close. I've spent a lifetime avoiding weaknesses my enemies could exploit."

Her chest felt tight. "You think I'd be a weakness?"

He tucked a strand of hair behind her ear. His voice lowered. "You already are."

A tremble went through her body. Dayna didn't think a man had ever made her tremble before. "I'm attracted to you."

"I'm attracted to you too. It's...inconvenient."

"That's one word for it," she muttered.

"I'm here to help and protect you."

She waved her hands at her body. "Not a child, Rillian."

"I'm well aware of that." His voice was low, his gaze intense. "For now, let's watch the fight."

Pulse pounding, she turned her head around to look

straight ahead. He led her down the stairs, and she studied the small crowd of people sitting near the railings circling the inner fight area. She sucked in a deep breath, glad to be outside, although a part of her missed the casino and the security it offered.

But she couldn't stay locked in her prison forever.

Her gaze fell on a group of women sitting together. Amongst them were a few large, bare-chested gladiators. As Dayna took the women in, her chest tightened. Her friends, her fellow people from Earth, and her fellow survivors.

One by one, they turned their heads and spotted her.

Smiles and cries broke out. Two women shot forward. Small, blonde Mia, and dark-haired Winter.

Dayna found herself engulfed by their sweet smells as they wrapped their arms around her. Warmth flooded her.

Mia pulled back, her face flushed. "It is so damn good to see you."

"So good," Winter said, smiling.

"How are you?" Mia demanded, holding Dayna's hand tightly.

"I'm okay." She saw the worry on their faces, and gave Mia another tight hug. No way was she going to go into detail about the hungry thing that lived inside her. "I'm dealing. It's been a lot to adjust to."

"You need to take your time." Winter patted Dayna's arm.

Dayna studied the lovely woman's face and her bi-colored eyes. Dayna remembered that terrible night that

Winter had been returned to their cell, sobbing and unable to see. "I am so glad you can see again, Winter."

Winter smiled. "Me, too. I can see perfectly well enough to smack my gladiator when he goes barbarian on me."

Dayna lifted her gaze, looking over the woman's head. The stone-faced Nero stood nearby, arms crossed over his muscled chest. The man looked...taciturn and grumpy. But when the gladiator's gaze slid toward Winter, Dayna watched it warm. She fought a smile. Clearly, Winter had taken down the big, barbarian gladiator.

She smiled, amused at the other humans, as well. She still couldn't believe that all of these women had found love with alien gladiators.

A hand pressed to the small of her back, sending electric shockwaves radiating through her.

"The fight's about to begin," Rillian drawled. "Take a seat."

"You're sitting with us." Mia tugged Dayna forward.

She followed, but glanced back. Rillian watched her for a moment, before he turned to talk with Galen.

Ignore it. Ignore him. Forcing her gaze off Rillian, she glanced at the imperator. Now there was an imposing man. The black eye patch over his left eye, and his rugged, scarred face were intimidating, along with the muscled body set off by a tight, black shirt and black cloak. Rillian was charm covering an edge of danger. Galen was raw power and authority.

"Here you go." A cup filled with a bunch of small

kernels was shoved into Dayna's hand. "*Mahiz*. Stuff is addictive."

Dayna smiled at Rory Fraser. The former space station engineer's red hair fell around her foxy face. She was munching on the snack and also rubbing her huge pregnant belly.

"How's life in the Dark Nebula Casino?" Winter asked.

"Screw the casino." Rory leaned forward. "How is it living with sex-on-a-stick Rillian?"

Dayna made a choking noise.

The redhead waved a hand in the air and gave an exaggerated shiver. "I have a super-hot gladiator baby daddy—" she patted her belly "—but Rillian..." She shivered again. "Just looking at that man is almost enough to induce multiple orgasms."

"Don't let Kace hear you say that." Regan, a former scientist from Fortuna, pushed her blonde hair over her shoulder.

Dayna burst into laughter and the rest of the women joined in. It felt so good to laugh and relax.

"So?" Rory said, raising a brow.

"He's an...interesting man," Dayna said.

Regan shook her head. "She's been working to get better, Rory. I'm sure she's not having a wild affair with the sexy casino owner." The pretty scientist was smiling.

Dayna managed a non-committal noise. "I won't lie, the man is far too easy to look at, but he's complicated."

"Sure is." Rory smiled. "And he looks at you like you're a tasty snack waiting to be devoured."

He does? Dayna's pulse jumped, and she turned to

look at the man in question. But suddenly, the small crowd started cheering.

"Here they come." Madeline, the former space station commander, leaned out over the railing.

Saved by the gladiators. Dayna turned, gripping the railing to look down into the arena. The sand was currently perfectly groomed, but she knew it wouldn't be long until it was disturbed by the fighters and splattered with blood. Kor Magna Arena didn't host fights to the death, but the gladiators still got hurt. That's why she knew the gladiatorial houses spent a fortune on the best medical tech.

She watched the House of Galen gladiators step out onto the sand.

There were lots of oiled muscles, black tattoos, and leather. Along with fascinating weapons. Dayna thoroughly enjoyed studying the swords, staffs, and axes that the gladiators carried.

Beside her, the women waved and whistled to the incoming gladiators.

Dayna watched the Kor Magna Champion, Raiden, stride out in the lead, his red cloak flaring behind him. By his side was Harper. Dayna couldn't believe the former space station security officer had become a gladiator. But Harper looked the part in tight fighting leathers and holding two swords.

The rest of the gladiators fanned out behind the couple.

The gladiators waved to the crowd. They seemed relaxed, and Dayna remembered this was an exhibition match against their strongest allies. There'd be no blood and no winner, just good sport.

"Galen," a deep, cool voice said from nearby.

Intrigued, Dayna turned, looking over her shoulder. She took in the man who'd just joined Rillian and Galen.

She stilled. The man had a powerful build, and short, dark hair. He wore black leathers, and one of his arms was made entirely of silver metal. As he turned his head, she saw another metal implant surrounding one of his eyes, which glowed a neon blue.

Cyborg. This had to be Magnus Rone, Imperator of the House of Rone.

"Now that is one scary dude," Mia murmured quietly.

Madeline leaned closer. "He met with Galen the other day. Magnus had some possible leads on Zaabha. Apparently, he was dropping a shipment of weapons—"

"Weapons?" Dayna interrupted.

Madeline nodded. "The House of Rone has expert weapons makers. They are renowned for their weapons. Anyway, Magnus went to take a shipment into the desert several weeks back, and ended up captured by desert slavers. He spent a few nights locked in a cage, before his gladiators rescued him."

"What idiot would capture Magnus Rone?" Mia mused.

"A very stupid one," Madeline continued. "When they captured him, they damaged his cyborg systems. He says he still hasn't got all his memories back from those few days. But recently, he remembered some snippets of conversations. About selling Earth women and about Zaabha."

Dayna straightened. God, maybe it could help them find Zaabha?

"So far, nothing's helped decode the map, but Galen's hoping Magnus will remember more," Madeline finished.

Mia glanced at the cyborg. "He seems so...cold. Like I said, scary dude."

Dayna bumped the woman with her shoulder. "You mated with one scary dude, remember."

The blonde smiled. "I sure did." Her gaze moved to the fighting floor.

Dayna followed her gaze, taking in the muscled, blue-skinned alien warrior. Dayna had first seen the wild fighter in the underground fight rings when she and Mia had been trapped in there. Now, he was Mia's mate.

The woman's smile was radiant. "He's wild and tough on the outside, but on the inside..." Her smile widened, then her gaze flicked back to the men behind them. "But Magnus, though? I'm not entirely sure that guy feels anything on the inside."

Dayna found her gaze drawn to Rillian. So cool and controlled. He smiled, he clearly enjoyed the best of everything, and his people respected him. But as far as she could see, the man held the world at arm's length, with the leash very much under his control.

There was another murmur from the crowd, followed by cheers. Dayna turned back to the arena, watching as the House of Rone gladiators stepped onto the sand.

"So, we're all coming to the Dark Nebula in a few days," Mia said, changing topics.

"Oh?"

Mia nodded. "Rillian is paying me a stupid amount of money to sing at a party." Mia frowned. "Although it sort of feels wrong to be partying when I know Ever and Sam are prisoners."

"We have to live," Dayna said. "You'll be great, Mia. Rillian only has the best in his casino."

A sly look crossed Mia's face. "Then that must be why he's looking at you like you're a particularly rare vintage of wine he wants to savor."

Again with the looking? Dayna shook her head, fighting not to glance back. "Now that all you guys have fallen in love, you're trying to pair off everybody else."

Mia grabbed Dayna's hand. "I just want you to be happy."

Dayna squeezed her friend's fingers. "I'm finding my way there." Suddenly, a siren sounded.

"Fight's starting," Rory said.

The gladiators met in a clash of swinging swords and axes. Dayna watched the fast, experienced moves, as the fighters ducked, weaved, and jumped.

Watching Harper leap into the air, Dayna gasped in awe. The woman twirled her twin swords in a deadly display, driving her opponent back. Regan's mate, Thorin, was all power as he slammed his giant axe down, cleaving off the handle of the axe of a rival gladiator.

All around, the crowd cheered and stomped their feet. Energy and excitement throbbed off the spectators and the fighters. It washed over Dayna.

She stilled, no longer seeing the fight in front of her. Every muscle in her body tightened, and she felt her symbiont stir. *No.*

The energy from the gladiators below was rich and strong. She watched Blaine, the sole human male survivor, thrusting with dual swords. His blades slammed against the staff of his rival. Sounds bombarded Dayna— the cheers, the hard grunts of the gladiators, heartbeats.

Panic flooded her. She felt her control slipping, drowning her in sensation. The stone in her chest started to burn.

Hungry.

She shot to her feet. She had to get away. She needed Rillian.

"Dayna?" Mia asked curiously.

Dayna looked at her friend. She could hear Mia's heartbeat. *Thump. Thump. Thump.* She felt the pure, fresh energy coming off the woman's small body.

She had to get out. She had to get away. Dayna took a step back.

Mia grabbed her arm and Dayna's vision turned red. *No!*

But it was too late.

Hungry. So hungry. Dayna lunged at Mia, knocking the smaller woman down onto the stone seat. She could hear her own voice screaming in her head, but she couldn't stop herself.

From somewhere down on the arena sand, she heard a wild roar. Shouts and screams echoed around them.

Dayna fought for control, her hands shaking. She stared down into Mia's startled face.

She's your friend. Protect her. A sob broke free. God, she couldn't stop herself. She held out a palm, reaching out to press it against Mia's chest.

With a roar, a blur of blue vaulted over the railing. Dark, swirling markings covered his skin and he snarled, his golden eyes fixed on Dayna.

Mia's mate let out a wild snarl and jumped into the air, going for Dayna's throat.

Suddenly, a black shadow leaped in front of Dayna, moving so fast she could barely track it.

Rillian appeared from nowhere, slamming into Vek, and knocking the alien gladiator back with alarming ease. Rillian turned, yanking Dayna off her feet and into his arms.

"She'll be fine." He strode away from the startled group.

Dayna controlled another sob, burying her face in Rillian's neck. She saw the gold glow of her symbiont stone through her shirt, and she knew her eyes would be glowing the same color.

"I'm not fine." She struggled against Rillian's hold.

They were halfway up the stairs and she managed to break free. She didn't look back at her friends, didn't want to see the horror on their faces. She ran.

She sprinted up the stairs two at a time and barreled into a tunnel. She had no idea where she was going, she just knew she had to get away from the energy of the crowd and away from the friends she'd failed.

Like she'd failed her sister.

She didn't want to hurt them.

With every step, she imagined the murderer who'd

stolen her sister, Gwendolyn. Dayna was supposed to be watching Gwen. Instead, a monster had taken a young, innocent child and broken her.

Dayna thought of Mia's frightened face. She was no better than that monster.

She came to a wide corridor that ringed the top of the arena. High, wide arches offered a stunning view of the city beyond. She ran right to the edge, pressing her toes over the drop and staring down. It would be a long, long fall to the ground below.

There was no sound behind her, but she knew he was there. Something in her sensed him.

"You want to jump?" Rillian drawled. "You want to end it?"

"I'm never going to adjust to this!" She pressed her palm to the burn in her chest.

"You will."

He stepped closer and she felt the heat of him right behind her.

"I've never met someone with such a strong will as yours," he said quietly.

"I wanted to absorb Mia's energy." Dayna squeezed her eyes closed, despair drenching her. "I wanted to drain her dry."

"It gets easier to control in time."

"I don't want to hurt anyone!"

A strong arm wrapped around her, and she felt a hand tangle in her hair. He tugged her back against his chest. "I won't let you."

She spun in his embrace and leaned into him.

Desperate for the feel of him, for his strength. Her hands gripped his shirt. "Hold me."

"I am."

She tried to burrow deeper. Then she looked up into liquid-silver eyes. "What if I hurt you?"

"You can't." A dark promise.

She held on tight. She leaned on his strength and didn't ever want to let go. Minutes ticked by, and she was suddenly aware of how close her lips were to his. Only a whisper apart.

The hungry, edgy feeling in her mutated into something else. Something far hotter and needier. Without a second thought, she went up on her toes and kissed him.

He didn't make a sound, but his arms tightened around her.

For a second, his lips remained motionless. Panic hit her. God, he was going to pull away...

Then his mouth took hers.

Oh. God. Sensation slammed into her. He angled his head, going deeper. It was hot and hard, like a blow crashing into her.

She slid a hand up, sliding it into his silky hair and pressed her body against his. This wasn't a kiss. This was a dark inferno swallowing her whole.

Suddenly, a discreet beeping noise penetrated the pleasure. Rillian broke the kiss, muttering a curse under his breath. He kept one arm around her as he pulled a small, sleek device from his pocket.

"Rillian," he answered, his voice was deep, with a husky edge.

"Sorry to bother you, Rillian."

Chest still heaving like she'd run a race, she recognized Tannon's deep voice.

"There's been another murder," the man said.

Dayna straightened and she felt Rillian stiffen.

"Where?" Rillian demanded.

"A body was left in your office."

"I'm on my way." Rillian slid the communicator away. His gaze fell on her. "Dayna."

His eyes were shuttered, completely unreadable. She swallowed, her belly still churning. She couldn't quite work out what he was thinking. Was this where he told her that kiss had been a mistake?

She cleared her throat. "I'm feeling better now. We should get to the Dark Nebula."

CHAPTER SIX

R illian stormed into his office.
One glance was all he needed to fully take in the long body draped over his desk.

The woman was wearing a blood-red catsuit made of a liquid fabric. Her dark, elaborate curls poured over his desk.

He cursed and then turned, kicking a chair and sent it skidding across his office floor.

"You knew her," Dayna said quietly.

"Yes."

She stepped closer and then she sucked in a breath. "God, it's the singer. The performer from the casino."

"Yes." Feeling helpless rage, Rillian stepped forward and gently closed the woman's eyes. "Her name was Illiana."

"She was your lover." Dayna's voice had gone cool.

"Former." They'd shared a few hot nights, but his

interest had cooled quickly, much to Illiana's dismay. She'd been ambitious.

She would have been horrified to hear that his kiss with Dayna Caplan was hotter than any of the nights he'd spent in Illiana's bed. He reached out and gripped Dayna's chin.

Her gaze met his.

"I haven't been with a woman for several months now. And the last few weeks, only one woman has been in my veins."

Emotion flickered in her eyes.

He released a breath, trying to keep a lid on his simmering desire. He let Dayna go. Now was not the time. Turning back to the desk, he shifted the mass of Illiana's hair.

Dayna made a sound. "You shouldn't mess with the scene until—"

He picked up the note written on heavy paper.

"What does it say?" she asked.

"Abandon your allies and take care of your own business. More bodies will follow."

Anger ignited like a torch in Rillian. He turned to the window, staring out at the city below. *You have made a very bad mistake.* His hand curled, crumpling the note.

"How did they get in?" Dayna mused.

"We don't know how they got in." This came from Tannon, standing in the doorway like a sentinel. "Security feed shows the victim arriving, but she was alone. Then the security feed was jammed. It only took a minute."

"Inside job?" Dayna's gaze narrowed.

Tannon straightened, his mouth a flat line. "My security team's been vetted, but we're checking."

"I only hire good people," Rillian added.

Dayna looked at him. "You know people, Rillian. You know desperation. Even the best, most-loyal person can be forced down a path they don't want to follow...if the incentive is right." Her gaze dropped to the dead woman. "Someone knows what they're doing."

"Maybe." Rillian blew out a breath, trying to find some measure of calm. If one of his own had betrayed him...

"My team is sending through the footage," Tannon said.

Rillian waved to the wall of screens, and Tannon murmured into his communicator. While they waited, Dayna peppered Tannon with a few pointed questions about entries, exits, and Illiana's location before the murder.

She knew what she was doing. Rillian watched her face come alive, and knew that this sort of work was in her blood. Something she'd clearly been missing. As his security head answered her questions, he saw the grudging respect grow on Tannon's face. Dayna was smart. Efficient.

Such a clever mind.

Funny that Rillian desired that mind as much as her strong, sexy body.

"So she was in her dressing room?" Dayna said.

"Yes," Tannon replied. "Watch." His dark gaze met Rillian's.

Seconds later, several screens flared to life. One

showed Illiana in her dressing room, primping at the mirror. There was a knock at the door, and a delivery woman carried in an enormous bouquet of rare alien flowers.

"Someone had flowers delivered to her," Tannon said, turning to Rillian. "From you."

"They were not from me," Rillian said.

"There was a note." A female security member was on the far screen. "Asking her to meet you in your office."

They watched Illiana's progress as she walked through the casino, smiling at people who stopped to shower her in praise. She took one of the elevators and the screen changed, showing her nodding at a security guard before entering Rillian's office.

The screen switched to the sole camera in his office. He saw Illiana do a sweep of the room, a private smile on her face.

Then the screen went blank.

His jaw clenched and he looked at the expensive timepiece on his wrist. Exactly a minute later, the screen blinked back to life, showing Illiana draped over his desk. Dead.

"She was poisoned," Tannon said. "Report from the initial scans just came in."

"How the *drak* did the killer get into my office?" Rillian's tone was ice-cold, but his symbiont stirred, reacting to his anger. He hired the best, for drak's sake.

Dayna stood, and circled the room, much as Illiana had. But instead of a pleased smile and a calculating look, Dayna's face was set in lines of concentration.

She walked past the glass, and then turned and

walked past it again. She swiveled, and did it a third time. It almost looked like she was pacing. Then she stopped and crouched.

She touched the glass with a long finger. "Here."

He moved in beside her and saw the neatly mended hole in the glass.

"God," she said. "Someone got into the tower from the *outside*."

"They flew," Rillian said grimly.

"All of this to get you to back off?" she said.

He gave her a single nod, heat spiking through his anger. "The Thraxians are running scared. They aren't thinking rationally anymore." His mouth flattened. "They miscalculated."

Rillian watched as Dayna studied the glass again, before she turned and crouched beside the body.

His anger was like a growing sandstorm. He hadn't lost control of his symbiont for years. Control was vital to him and his symbiont was far too dangerous. His hands curled into fists. He *had* to keep his control.

If not, he'd be the most dangerous, unstoppable predator that Kor Magna had ever seen.

His gaze fell on Dayna. He found himself fascinated by the look on her face. He had no trouble remembering the feel of her, the taste of her.

Rillian's anger receded. He took some deep breaths.

He wanted her taste in his mouth again. He wanted to taste more of her. He wanted to sink his teeth into her and devour her.

No. Turning, he stared out the window and ground his teeth together.

She was fighting her symbiont every step of the way. She still had a way to go before she was even close to accepting her new reality. Dayna Caplan was stubborn and strong. Fiercely intelligent, and not easy at all.

As he turned back to the murdered woman on his desk, it was the image of Dayna burned into his brain... and the knowledge that it wasn't just the murders stroking his symbiont to lose control.

It was his reaction to Dayna.

Maybe Tannon was right. Maybe Dayna was the greatest risk of all.

———

AN HOUR LATER, Rillian's security team had finished their analysis of the scene and removed Illiana's body. A cleaning crew had just finished, and his office looked pristine, as usual.

He didn't feel so calm.

He moved over to the drinks cabinet on the far wall, and pulled out a bottle of Dark Fire whiskey. He poured the glittering black liquid into a glass just as Dayna entered.

She looked miserable.

He held the glass out to Dayna. "You look like you could use this."

"No, thanks." She shook her head, returning her gaze to the painting on the wall. "I just got off a call with Mia."

He lifted the glass and knocked the drink back in a quick move. Dark Fire couldn't be tolerated by many species, and he enjoyed the fiery burn. "She was upset."

"Yes. For *me*. She apologized to *me*." Dayna shook her head.

"But you wanted her to yell and cry? To help you beat yourself up a bit more?"

Dayna shot him a glare.

"You have good friends, Dayna, and they care about you. That's a rare thing."

She nodded, her gaze still on the painting. "It's striking."

He stared at the bright splashes of color on black. "I like striking things." His gaze moved over her. "I like the bold, the unusual."

She turned, her face considering. "The Thraxians aren't so discerning." A faint shiver was the only give-away about how the Thraxians affected her. "They're bold and in-your-face. They're not subtle or sneaky."

He lowered his glass, following her train of thought. "Cunning, sneaky murders aren't the way they operate."

She nodded. "That's right. These murders feel...more personal."

Rillian scowled. "It has to be the Thraxians. My team has found Thraxian biomatter on the notes."

"Then they've recruited someone else, someone who knows you, to help with this."

No one knew Rillian. He preferred it that way. He blew out a breath, pouring one last shot of whiskey. His anger was too close to the surface, his control too shaky. The symbiont running along his spine throbbed, amplifying his emotions.

He needed to work it off before he got too close to

losing his control. That was the one thing he would never allow.

"I'm going to work out in my gym." He'd dial up the hardest program on his holo-sparring system.

Dayna watched him steadily, like she could see right into his head. "I'm sorry, Rillian. About Illiana."

"A waste of a life and her talent."

"Is that all she was to you?"

"We enjoyed each other, briefly. That was it." He swirled the last of his drink.

"Because you don't let people too close."

He lifted his gaze to meet hers. "My life is exactly how I like it."

"Glossy, opulent, and distant."

He tilted his head, setting the glass down and stepping closer to her. "I like it under my control."

"You can't control everything. You keep people at arm's length. I wonder why?"

His body brushed hers. "You're not at arm's length."

She blinked, as though suddenly realizing that she'd been cornered by a predator. "Rillian—"

He backed her against the wall, cupping her jaw. "Don't analyze me, Dayna."

She lifted her chin. "So you're allowed to see all my weaknesses, but I don't get a glimpse of yours?"

A voice in his head told him that he should back away, but something about her drew him. For once in his life, he wasn't exactly sure what he was doing.

"Back off." She shoved against his chest.

"No. I don't think so." The turbulent feelings inside him swelled, and Rillian did the one thing he never did—

he stopped thinking. He lowered his head until his mouth was a whisper from hers.

She stilled, her gaze dropping to his lips. "What do you want from me?"

He hadn't worked it out yet. But he reached for her. He needed to touch her.

Rillian slammed his mouth down on hers, absorbing the taste of her. The scent of her hit him, and he slid a hand under her shirt, feeling her unbelievably smooth skin.

She moaned into his mouth, kissing him back. Her tongue tangled with his.

Desire exploded inside Rillian—hot and strong. His cock was hard as a rock, pushing against his trousers. The strength of his need almost brought him to his knees.

He wanted to possess her. Push her down and simply mount her, slide his cock inside her so they'd be joined.

Shock rippled through him. He never felt like this. It had to be his symbiont. That *had* to be it.

He yanked back from her. The room was quiet, except for their ragged breathing.

"That was...ill-advised," he managed.

"Probably." She stepped closer and went up on her toes. She wound her arms around his neck, and kissed him again.

With a growl, he wrapped an arm around her, walking her across the room. *Take. Claim. Mate.*

He didn't have time for foreplay or exploration. Right now, all he needed was to be lodged inside her. For Rillian, sex was usually a hot, elegant dance. But this... this was something entirely different.

He pushed her against the desk, lifting her up, his hands sliding up to cup her breasts. She arched into his caress, one of her legs wrapping around his hips.

"Yes." Her voice was a husky whisper.

He wanted her. Right here. On his desk.

At the same moment, they both froze. *Drak.* On the desk where a dead woman had been left as a warning.

They pulled apart.

Dayna stood, touching her lips. "God, you scramble my brain."

Drak. Drak. Rillian's control was a precarious thing. A very male, very primitive part of him just wanted to drag her down onto the floor and pound inside her.

It had been many years since he'd felt so out of control. He'd fought to make his life exactly as he wanted it, where his control was absolute. So no one would ever take advantage of him again.

This woman was dangerous. Especially when he was in a dangerous mood.

"I have to go," he said.

Surprise flashed on her face. "Oh." She tucked a strand of her glossy, brown hair behind her ear.

His gaze dropped to her lips. They were swollen from his kisses, and the sight of that made his cock pulse.

"Rillian?"

Drak it all. Rillian turned, strode out, and pretended that he wasn't escaping.

CHAPTER SEVEN

D ayna paused in the doorway of the gym, watching Rillian sparring against what looked like an entire gang of fighters.

The faint flicker in the men made her realize that they were some sort of solid holograms.

Rillian shifted and dodged with a fluid grace that made her mouth go dry. He was shirtless, wearing a soft pair of black workout trousers. His muscles flexed, and he landed hard blows, spun, and kicked out powerfully. His holographic opponents blinked out as he struck them. He swiveled, bringing his fists up to hit again.

The man was gorgeous.

It was one thing to have an attractive package, it was another to know how to use it.

Dayna let herself admit the full extent of her attraction. The times she and Rillian had kissed, she'd felt...alive.

For the first time in a very long time, she'd thought

nothing of aliens, pain, captivity, and nightmares. She'd felt like a woman and she'd felt like something in her life finally made sense.

He wasn't as bulky as the gladiators. His chest was lean with delineated muscles, and his abdomen was tight and ridged. She pulled in an unsteady breath. He'd have no trouble swinging a sword, if he wanted to.

She watched him spin, then leap high, delivering a powerful front kick. He took down another opponent, but a second slipped in from the side and landed a blow to Rillian's lower back.

He stumbled and let out a hiss. She realized then that the program delivered some sort of pain response when a hit connected.

Rillian made a sound and took the fighter down with a hard chop. He paused, heaving in air, and turned.

That's when she got a clear view of his muscled back...and the symbiont lying along his spine. She let out a sharp gasp.

God. It looked like an alien creature that had burrowed into his skin. It glowed a bright silver-blue.

She felt an answering throb in the stone on her chest. They both had these alien lifeforms that were now a part of them.

Suddenly, he turned, his gaze on her. "I'm not in a good mood."

Dayna toed off her shoes and moved onto the mat. "I don't mind. You don't have to be glossy, suave Rillian for me all the time."

He frowned at her, lowering into a stretch. She moved over to study the fancy fight-simulation controls on the console beside the mat. "How do you make a holo-gram solid?"

"Ultrasonic technology that creates touchable force fields." He stretched his arm, his biceps flexing. "The program projects sound waves that create a sensation of touch."

"I'd love to test it out." She'd been using the gym a lot the last few weeks, but had no idea about the holographic simulation. It had been far too long since she'd flexed her martial arts skills.

He shot her an unreadable look, then moved to touch the controls.

Around her, lights whirled, and several brutish-looking aliens appeared. They were covered in scales, with sharp claws, and each towered over her by at least a foot. She moved into a fighting stance and raised her arms. The first alien attacked and she leaped forward to meet him.

As she ducked, kicked, and hit, Dayna felt her muscles warm-up. She dodged and landed several good blows. One of her opponents blinked out. She smiled. *Take that, asshole.* Working across the mat, completely absorbed in the fight, she took out another target.

The last fighter rushed at her. She blocked, but he got a punch in and she felt an electric shock vibrate through her. She gritted her teeth. *Ouch.* Motivated, she swung her leg, landing a hard kick to the alien's gut. He staggered, and she slammed an elbow into his face. His image dissolved.

She straightened, grinning. A light sheen of sweat covered her skin.

"Ready for more?" Rillian asked.

"Bring it."

A large mob of different aliens blinked into existence. Rillian strode out to the center of the mat and stood beside her.

As the fighters rushed at them, Dayna and Rillian exploded into action.

They moved together. She brought one big alien down, and Rillian swung in behind her to protect her back, while slamming an unforgiving fist into the face of another attacker.

Finding a rhythm, they worked together to plow through their opponents. Between blows, Dayna let out a laugh. God, this was *fun*. She hit a smaller alien in the chest, and when she spun around, two more were coming at her. Big brutes. *Shit*.

Rillian slammed into one, but she couldn't avoid the fist of the other. It rammed into her jaw.

She staggered backward, electric pain zapping her. "Ow." She kicked out, and the alien winked out of existence.

There were no more left.

Rillian gave her a small smile, one that held a dangerous edge. She felt the hairs on the back of her neck rise.

He touched the controls. "I'm moving it up to the next level. Think you can keep up?"

She narrowed her gaze. "Don't worry about me. But if you can't keep up, I'll compensate."

That dangerous smile again.

Opponents appeared, and they didn't pause, rushing

in fast. Dayna immediately lost herself in the fight, anticipating Rillian's moves. She ducked under his arm, ramming an uppercut into an alien's stomach. These fighters all moved faster, hit harder. She and Rillian both swiveled, landing twin back kicks to another pair of fighters. Then, as Rillian bent low, she rolled over his back, legs swinging as she kicked an incoming fighter.

Soon, Dayna was sweating. Her shirt was damp, and loose strands of her hair stuck to her forehead. She ducked a fighter's arm, then swung out with her foot, before she followed up with a hard punch.

Finally, they took the last opponent down. Dayna leaned forward, pressing her hands to her knees.

Rillian turned to pick up a towel that had been set out on a bench and wiped his face. Once again, her gaze moved to his symbiont, and the muscled back it was attached to.

He glanced over his shoulder and caught her looking. He turned to give her a better view.

"Sorry," she murmured, grabbing herself a towel.

"Don't be. Feel free to look."

Unable to stop herself, she moved closer. She wanted to touch it, but she wasn't sure she could. But Rillian stayed still, and she lifted a hand. She gently touched the muscle beside his spine. The creature looked embedded to his spine. She lightly touched the symbiont, and he tensed.

She froze. "Does it hurt?"

"No." His voice held a low, husky edge.

It looked like it was made from bony cartilage and filled with silver-blue fluid.

"It's known as a Vraskan symbiont. A lifeform from a mostly uncharted star system far from here. They are extremely painful when they attach, and kill most of their hosts."

She hissed out air. "But you survived."

"I did."

"And my symbiont?"

"I haven't seen one exactly like yours before, but I've seen similar ones. It's native to Carthago, and like mine, feeds on energy."

Then he pulled away. Damn, the man was so hard to get a read on. Dayna was used to utilizing her observation skills to get a gauge of people and what they were feeling. Rillian confounded her.

But from what she could tell, he was angry. At the murders, or perhaps at this desire simmering between them.

"Want to fight me now?" She set her towel down.

He spun, brow furrowed. "I don't think—"

God, that face. "Well, if you're afraid..." She shrugged a shoulder.

Silver sparked in his eyes and he dropped his towel. "Bring it on, Earth woman."

"Sure thing, Slick."

They moved onto the mats and started trading some easy kicks and hits. But she knew he'd never work his anger off with a few easily-blocked kicks.

Dayna decided to fight dirty. She'd learned a few tricks training with her fellow police officers. You didn't make it on the streets without knowing a few.

She dropped low, chopping her hand against his

thigh. She unconsciously pulled on some of the enhanced strength of her symbiont.

He grunted and staggered. Then, with a growl, he came after her. She spun away and felt the rush of air as he swung at her. She blocked the hit, gritting her teeth as it rattled through her. She turned and he matched her, their bodies brushing. She jabbed an elbow into his ribs.

Dayna felt strength coursing through her. Maybe this part of having a symbiont wasn't so bad.

As she and Rillian danced across the mats, she saw more silver bleed into his eyes. *Kick. Chop. Punch.* They spun yet again, and she found herself pressed up against him. She smelled healthy male sweat and the dark spice of his cologne.

And she sensed the energy of him. Bright, hot, and jagged.

"The symbiont enhances your anger," she said.

"Sometimes. It doesn't generate feelings, only amplifies them." He spun away, and they moved back across the mats in a series of hits and kicks.

Then Dayna changed things up. She leaped at him, taking him by surprise. Her knees hit his torso, and when they landed on the mat, she was straddling his chest.

Gripping his wrists, she tried to slam them over his head.

But he was too strong. She shoved, but he moved, his palms pressing against hers.

"That anger will eat you up if you let it," she said. "You need to let it go. I know what it's like to find dead bodies, to know that you were too late to save them. To know that there'll be more."

"I never let go." He pushed up, rolling her across the mat. They wrestled and she scissored her legs, trying to get on top again.

"It isn't good to hold it in," she panted.

"You don't know what you're talking about."

Suddenly, he pushed at her with a huge wave of strength. Her back slammed onto the mat, and she ended up with a furious male on top of her. God, he was so much stronger than she'd thought. He'd been holding back all this time. His face was close to hers, set in harsh lines.

One of his hands circled her throat, his fingers pressing to her pulse point. His eyes were pure molten silver.

She went still. She'd driven him to lose his control.

Then she felt a sharp tug in her chest. Sensation spread through her. He was pulling at her energy. *No.*

He was feeding from her.

Fear shot through her. She remembered the desert witch feeding from her. Pain, horror, and helplessness.

"No!" She shoved against him, her body going wild as she struggled.

All of sudden, Rillian went stiff and cursed. He released her, and then his body was gone from hers.

Shakily, she sat up, pushing her sweaty hair off her face.

He was facing away from her, his back stiff and his symbiont glowing. "I'm sorry."

"It's...okay."

"No, it isn't. You were right, Dayna. My symbiont likes more than just energy."

83

"What?" she asked quietly, a sense of dread washing over her.

"My symbiont likes to kill." His face was the hardest she'd ever seen it.

Horror slammed into her. In her head, she saw her sister's murdered body.

Rillian's eyes flashed. Like he knew exactly what she was thinking. All emotion bled out of his face. "Yes, back on Earth, I'd be a monster you'd lock away. Don't push me again, Dayna. You're here to learn, so let that be a lesson for you." His voice was as cold as ice.

Then he turned and left her there.

Dayna collapsed back on the mats. God, when had her life become so damn complicated? She ran a shaky hand over her chest. She felt a pulse of energy from her symbiont and this time, she didn't block it or ignore it.

Abduction, captivity, torture, host to an alien symbiont, and completely lusting after a dangerous, powerful, and complex alien man who just admitted he could be a killer.

No. Rillian ruthlessly controlled everything, including his symbiont. He took care of his employees, he allied with the House of Galen to help others, and he didn't let anyone close.

Except her.

He was no killer.

CHAPTER EIGHT

Sweaty from the gym, Dayna headed back to her bedroom. She'd spent several hours in her office frustrating herself that Zaabha seemed more elusive than ever. Then she'd worked herself pretty hard in the gym, trying not to think of a certain wealthy casino owner.

She thought again of the moment he'd started to feed on her energy and rubbed her symbiont stone. She also thought of what she'd almost done to Mia.

Dayna stopped, dropping back against the wall. It was time. She couldn't ignore this alien inside her any more.

She needed to learn to feed.

Her stomach twisted and she headed back down the hall. Sleep first, then she'd think about that in the fresh light of day. Using her enhanced hearing, and accessing some of those abilities her symbiont gave her, she listened to the noise on the penthouse level.

No other sound except the rush of air from the ventilation. Rillian must be down in the casino somewhere.

When she stepped into her bedroom, she saw the small communications device on her bed. Frowning, she snatched it up.

"Dayna," Rillian's rich voice filled the room. "Tannon has a lead. Exactly twenty minutes ago, the Thraxian who left the biomatter on the notes from the murders entered the Dark Nebula. We've been unable to find him, but we tracked him to a new nightclub I have opening tonight. I thought you'd like to be there."

"You thought right." She hurried to the bathroom.

"There's a dress hanging in your closet. You'll need to fit in and not scare him off."

Dayna pulled a face.

"I also left you another gift you might like."

She pulled another face. "It had better not be sparkly." She spotted the box on her bedside table. It wasn't a huge box, but it was too big for jewelry.

Pulling the lid off, she paused, a smile stretching over her face.

He'd given her a laser pistol.

She pulled the matte-black weapon from the box. It fit perfectly in her hands. Just the right size and weight.

Damn the man. He apparently had her all worked out. She also found a sexy little thigh holster, small enough to wear under a dress.

She hurried to get ready. In record time, she was speed walking down the corridor to the elevators, smoothing her hand down the short skirt of her dress. It was just loose enough to hide her new pistol that was strapped to her thigh.

She stroked the glossy fabric. It was black, but when she moved, tiny shots of silver filaments were visible. It reminded her of Rillian's eyes. The gown had a high neck that tied at her shoulder, and the back...was non-existent. Her legs were also mostly bare.

She felt incredibly uncomfortable and sexy at the same time.

When she reached the elevator, Rillian was leaning against the wall beside it.

Liquid-silver eyes moved over her, a flash of heat making them glow. "Perfect."

Dayna was still trying to get her breath back. He wore a tailored black suit, with a coat that fell to his knees. His shirt was so white that it looked silver. He was so damn handsome that he stole her breath.

He held out an arm for her and she slid hers through his. "Any sign of the Thraxian?"

Rillian shook his head. "He's being very sneaky for a drakking Thraxian. The nightclub is packed. He's there, but no one's seen him yet."

Sounded extremely fishy to her. As they stepped into the elevator, she studied Rillian's face. "Are you still angry?"

"No. I'm in perfect control."

She once again found that handsome face unreadable. "I do not think you are a killer."

He touched the elevator controls. "Then you're foolish."

She shrugged. "You aren't going to scare me off with the icy-cold Rillian routine. I know you."

His gaze zeroed in on her face.

"I know you," she said again. "And I don't mean the mask you show the world."

The elevator whizzed them downward, but this time, they stopped at one of the middle levels of the building. As he led her into a plush-carpeted corridor lined by magnificent art that made her think of nebulas and distant planets, she heard the muted thump of music ahead.

"By the way, thank you for the laser pistol."

He smiled. "I thought it suited you better than jewels."

At a large doorway, they paused, and she took in the packed room.

"Welcome to Darkest Sin," he drawled.

The new club was dark, sexy, and expensive. It suited him.

The walls were black, and the ceiling looked like liquid silver. Giant chandeliers draped down and lights pulsed to the music. Through a wall of glass, she saw a large terrace extending off the side of the building, filled with intimate tables, chairs, and couches.

Gorgeous men and women were packed on the dance floor, gyrating. Several servers walked through the crowd with trays full of multi-colored drinks. All of them didn't just wear silver, but looked like they'd been dipped in the metal. They were covered in head-to-toe silver paint.

Rillian tugged her forward, and they descended the black steps and moved into the crowd. She watched people react to him. A small ripple went through the crowd and women eyed him hungrily.

For many of the women, Dayna knew it was about his wealth and position. But for her, it was the irresistible pull of the man. It wasn't just the glossy looks, it was the intelligent mind and the single-minded dedication to running his empire.

It was also the fact that he'd felt anger and grief over the death of an employee he didn't know and a former lover. She'd talked enough to his staff to know he took care of his own. It was also because he held himself back from the world, not letting it get close enough to ruffle him.

He deserved to be ruffled. She knew life couldn't be lived properly if you didn't get your feet dirty sometimes.

God, she wanted him. She was tired of fighting her desire. For once, she wanted pleasure. On her own terms. She wanted Rillian.

She was quiet as he checked in with his people. He talked with the club manager, a blue-skinned woman wearing a silver shirt with her tailored trousers. After ensuring that everything was running smoothly, he found Tannon standing by the bar.

For once, the taciturn security man looked relaxed and was nursing a drink. She realized he was blending in.

"Any sign of our visitor?" Rillian murmured.

Tannon shook his head. "Nothing." Frustration twisted his lips. "I don't know how he could be a drakking ghost."

"We'll find him." With a nod, Rillian pulled Dayna deeper into the club.

"Drink?" he asked.

She shook her head. Rillian was intoxicating enough.

"There are a few guests I need to greet."

She stood beside him as he stopped to talk with a few people she guessed were Kor Magna VIPs. They all eyed her curiously while she covertly scanned the room.

She didn't see any Thraxians. No towering bodies, or black horns, or dark, cracked skin with orange glowing beneath.

He finally pulled her away. "Dance with me?"

She blinked up at him. "Dance? Right now?"

"He could be hiding on the dance floor."

Rillian pulled her into the center of the dance floor and Dayna's pulse skipped. The music throbbed, the beat moving through her. The sounds were alien, but the beat of a song always felt familiar. She'd always enjoyed dancing on the rare times she managed to make it out with friends. Usually they hit the pub, but occasionally they made it to a club of some sort.

Rillian pulled her closer, swaying to the music. Her body brushed against his, and before she knew it, they were pressed together. The music echoed in her ears and the heat of him warmed her skin. His arms wrapped around her and he fitted one leg between hers. Desire. It flared to life, urgent, insistent.

She forced herself to remember why they were there. She scanned the dance floor, taking in the writhing mass.

"Rillian."

She heard Tannon's tinny voice. Rillian was wearing some sort of earpiece.

"Go ahead," Rillian answered.

"The Thraxian biosignature has disappeared."

Rillian muttered a curse. "He left?"

"It appears that way. My team is doublechecking."

Dayna muttered a few curses of her own. At this rate, they'd never find Zaabha.

"Well, we may as well enjoy the music," Rillian said.

Sure. She kept moving to the song, but she thought of Ever and Sam. They sure as hell weren't dancing.

But it wasn't long before the music worked its way through her system and she felt her muscles relax. The press of Rillian's strong body was too tantalizing to ignore.

She remembered his fingers on her throat earlier in the gym, the feel of energy being pulled from her.

What she hadn't registered at the time was that when he'd done that, it had felt good. She swallowed. Now she was curious as to what a proper feeding might feel like.

Rillian moved with the beat, although he didn't use fancy dance moves. They just swayed against each other, feeling the energy, the music, and the crowd work through them.

She leaned into him. She could hear his steady heartbeat. His hand slid up her back, pressing against her skin. His touch left a heated trail.

She moved against him. "Rillian—"

He stroked lower, until his fingers touched the lower back of her dress, just above her ass, rubbing the delicate skin there. An intimate caress. His fingers slipped inside the fabric, cupping her ass.

"You drive me out of my mind," he murmured against her ear. "No one ever has before."

God. She rubbed against him, feeling the hard erection in his trousers. He spun her, until her back was pressed to his chest. The crowd was close, other bodies bumping against them. The music changed, and the lights dimmed. They were mostly drenched in shadow, with the odd burst of colored light here and there.

"You need someone to shake you out of your neat, controlled life," she said.

Rillian's hand slipped up her thigh, and she felt it go under the hem of her dress, bunching the fabric of her dress up. "Is that right?"

She gasped and grabbed his wrist. "Yes."

"You're already shaking me up and all I want is more." Hot lips pressed against her neck.

She arched back against him. Then she released his hand. His clever fingers continued moving under her dress. He stroked the weapon strapped to her thigh. "This is sexier than seeing Friskan diamonds against your skin."

Dayna swallowed. She hadn't bothered with panties. The dress was cut too low at the back. "No one ever says no to you or pushes you."

"It's dangerous to push me, Dayna." His fingers slid between her legs and when he realized she was bare, she heard him groan. He stroked her folds.

Oh, God. He was stroking her right here in the middle of a crowded room. "You don't frighten me."

"I should," he growled against her ear. "And I shouldn't want you this much."

"But you do," she panted.

"Yes." One thick finger slid inside her.

As the music thumped around them, Rillian worked her. She leaned back into him, and a second finger joined the first. She stifled a moan. His fingers found a rhythm and then his thumb rubbed her clit.

Jesus, she was going to come. She felt her body tense, and she gripped onto his wrist. He tilted her head back, his mouth covering hers. He kissed her deeply, and with another stroke, Dayna came. Sensation flooded her, making her body shake. He swallowed her cries with his mouth.

She collapsed against him. God, little shivers of pleasure still coursed through her.

"I shouldn't be touching you."

"I know what I want."

"You have no idea what I want to do to you." His dark voice made her shiver. "I'm trying to do the right thing. For both of us."

She spun to face him. "Rillian, I am not some weak damsel in need of protection. I can make my own decisions."

"Enough." He stepped back from her. "Go to your room and—"

"Like a child? The all-powerful Rillian always knows best."

"Don't push me, Dayna," he warned.

"I told you, I think you need it."

He leaned in, his voice harsh. "I know what I need." Then he turned and stalked off into the crowd.

Dayna closed her eyes. She didn't feel like dancing anymore. She climbed the steps to exit, but something made her look back.

Rillian had been mobbed by the crowd. He stood in the center of the club, and had two women clinging to him. On one side was a voluptuous blonde, and on the other, a svelte blue-haired woman.

Dayna's belly clenched. She watched him lean over, a faint smile on his face, as he touched a strand of the blonde's hair and tucked it behind her ear.

And then without lifting his head, his gaze flicked up and met Dayna's.

Bastard. If he wanted easy and safe, he could have it.

Lifting her chin, she turned and walked out. But as she strode down the corridor, she fisted a hand and pressed it to her aching chest.

RILLIAN HAD SLEPT BADLY.

He finished dressing, fastening his shirt. He'd forced himself to stay at the club long enough not to have people gossiping over his departure. He'd smiled and listened, but all his thoughts had been focused on Dayna and what they'd done on the dance floor. Finally, he'd shaken off the partygoers and left.

Dayna had pushed at him, challenged him. And he'd snapped and taken his bad mood out on her. In the morning light, he was feeling better physically. His symbiont had settled, and his anger had cooled.

He stared at his reflection in the mirror. It was easy to see the scrappy con artist and smuggler he'd once been. He realized he looked a lot like the mother who'd essentially abandoned him and left him to rot. She'd died a bloody death several years ago, but he guessed she lived on in the son she'd mostly ignored.

He'd fought hard to get where he was, and it had been a long time since anyone had made him react on instinct.

Leaving his room, he went looking for Dayna. He figured he owed her an apology.

He knocked on her bedroom door and didn't wait for an answer, but just pushed it open.

Her room was empty and her bed was neatly made. His gut clenched. His efficient cleaning staff wouldn't have been in yet. Drawing a breath, he picked up Dayna's scent—faded and several hours old.

She hadn't slept in her room.

He spun, panic trickling into his veins. Where was she? Where had she spent the night? His jaw tightened, remembering the furious look she'd shot him at the party. *Who* had she spent the night with?

Storming into his office, he went to his screens. She had to be here somewhere. She was still afraid of her symbiont. She wouldn't have left.

Then he scented her.

He turned and walked through the adjoining door to the conference room. He pulled up short.

She was asleep in a chair.

Slowly he walked over and sat in the chair across from her. There were papers spread on the table, and the comp screen was glowing. He saw Illiana's autopsy report, and the text of the Zaabha map. He'd had Tannon translate everything into Dayna's home language for her. Looking back at Dayna's relaxed face, he sat there for a moment and watched her sleep.

Those pretty, intelligent eyes were closed, but even in sleep, she still had a stubborn tilt to her jaw.

"Dayna."

She startled awake. "I was just resting my eyes."

He smiled. "Really?"

"Yes." Her gaze came into focus and landed on him. Then it cooled. "Did you enjoy your evening?"

He ignored the venom in her voice. "No."

She leaned over to shuffle the papers on the table.

"I spent most of it in the security room," he told her.

She shrugged, like she didn't care.

"I'm...sorry for yesterday evening." Her gaze met his again. "I was angry and I took it out on you."

She stared at his face before her tight shoulders relaxed a little. "I was planning to stay angry at you a while longer yet."

"I didn't enjoy any of those women. I worked with Tannon most of the night and we learned that the Thraxian had left his biomatter on a dagger. He had someone sneak it into the party and leave it behind."

"Toying with us."

Rillian nodded and raked a hand through his hair. "I warned you that me losing control is not a good idea."

She tilted her head. "Because of your symbiont."

He nodded. "I was never supposed to survive my symbiont. They almost always kill their hosts and they are very powerful."

She tilted her head. "If you lose control?"

"Then my symbiont will go on a feeding rampage."

"Oh."

"Yes, oh. So you see why I don't lose control. Plus, I don't like it."

She managed a small smile. "You're going to have to accept that you're mortal like the rest of us, Rillian."

He smiled. "Shh, don't tell anyone."

That startled a laugh out of her. Then there was a knock at the door and one of the kitchen staff rolled in a tray covered in food.

"Breakfast, sir."

"Thank you, Drast."

Dayna groaned. "Feeding me again."

The man set the food on the conference table and left. Rillian loaded up a plate and set it in front of Dayna. "I've spent a lot of time working out what suits the human palate best." He smiled. "And what you like."

She plucked up a piece of fruit. "I know. No one's ever looked after me before."

"What about your parents?"

She shrugged. "After my sister died, they were pretty messed up. I took over a lot of the household chores. And after my mom died—" another shrug "—I just kept doing them."

From a little girl, she'd been responsible and taking care of everyone else. It just made him want to spoil her more.

They ate together, Dayna pulling sheets of paper for perusal as she popped various bits of food in her mouth. She paused, her eyes fluttering as she absorbed the tastes.

He watched her lips. He could watch her eat all day.

"We need to find Zaabha." She leaned back in her

chair. "If we want to stop the murders, we need to stop the reason the Thraxians are killing people. We need to be on the offense, not the defense."

Rillian sipped some *zava* juice. It was tart and sweet. "I prefer action. To find Zaabha, we need to solve the witch's map."

"You said Galen's had people go over it?"

"Yes. Nothing."

"Maybe we should talk to Neve and Corsair? They found it, and might know more if we ask the right questions."

"A good idea. I'll contact them and ask them to come here."

He saw that she was now picking at the food, where moments before she'd been eating with gusto. A grimace crossed her face, and she dropped a hand to rub the spot where her symbiont lived.

"You need to feed," he said quietly.

She pushed her chair back. "Maybe. Probably. Yes. But I'm not quite ready, yet."

He nodded, seeing the glow in her eyes. "You can't leave it for much longer." He stood. "I'll contact Corsair."

Back in his office, Rillian asked his assistant to contact the caravan master. Then he started taking care of some business that had been building up. He made several calls, gave lots of orders, and arranged some meetings for his Dark Oasis Project.

As he stared out the window, his gaze moved to the edge of the desert, and he thought of the human women still lost out there—Ever and Sam. He hoped they were still alive. Still the same as they had been.

He pulled his sleek comp screen closer and tapped it. Immediately, it filled with camera feed of Dayna sitting in the adjacent conference room.

She was rubbing her lower back. He knew that the chairs weren't made for extended use, and made a mental note to order a more comfortable one for her. But she ignored her aches, leaned over and jotted down some notes. Resilient and tough. Beautiful and smart. His fingers curled around the screen. By the stars, he wanted her.

His communicator beeped. "Sir?" His assistant's modulated voice. "Caravan Master Corsair for you."

"Thank you, Tarin. Put him through."

Time to find Zaabha.

CHAPTER NINE

"What's a girl got to do to get some food around here?" Dayna hitched herself up on the glossy countertop in the casino's main kitchen.

"Go, you're invading my space." Chef Derol brought down a knife, chopping open a bright-red fruit called *heppla*.

Dayna grinned at him. "We both know you like it."

He made a harrumphing sound. Then he handed her a piece of the fruit. "The boss ordered more *heppla* for you, even though it's out of season. He noticed you like them."

Hmm. She took the piece, popped it in her mouth, and moaned. "He notices everything."

A wide smile graced Derol's narrow face. "He does. Especially when a beautiful woman is involved."

She snatched up another piece of fruit and shot the chef a sour look. "He has lots of beautiful women around him."

Another deft move of the knife. "I should have said a beautiful, smart, and interesting woman."

She grinned. "Charmer."

"Preparing a big feast for the party tonight." Derol started chopping again.

"My friend is singing." Dayna fiddled with a slice of *heppla*. God, she hoped Mia had truly forgiven her after the episode at the fight. She blew out a breath.

Then the chef looked past her, going quiet. She turned her head and spotted Tannon, looking grimmer than usual.

"Dayna, Rillian asked me to find you. Caravan Master Corsair and Neve are here."

Her heart leaped, and she jumped off the counter. "Thanks, Derol."

"*Chef* Derol."

She blew him a kiss, watching his cheeks turn dull red and his chest puff up. Then she was headed for the elevators with Tannon. As usual, the ride was silent. Tannon was not a stunning conversationalist.

Soon, she was striding down the hall to Rillian's office.

When she stepped inside, she instantly saw the couple standing on the other side of Rillian's big desk.

Rillian sat back in his chair, as elegant and controlled as always. Instead, Dayna focused on the visitors. Their pale, desert clothes should have looked out-of-place in the Dark Nebula, but they suited the pair.

Neve Haynes was a striking woman with an athletic body, long, black hair, and skin many shades darker than Dayna's. She turned, her gaze settling on Dayna. She had pale-green eyes that didn't miss much. Dayna knew the woman had been a corporate spy prior to her abduction.

"How are you, Dayna?" Neve asked.

"Alive," Dayna answered. "Free." Mostly. She ignored the tightening in her chest, and moved forward.

Dayna looked at the man at Neve's side. Compared to Rillian, the two men were night and day. The casino owner and caravan master. One was long, lean, and dark, the other was tall, muscular, and tawny. One elegance personified, while the other one had a rough, wild edge. Suave and polished contrasted against roguish adventurer.

"Dayna, it's good to see you looking so well," Corsair said with a smile.

"Thank you," she said. "And thank you again for rescuing me from the witch."

He inclined his head, his hand reaching for Neve's. "No one deserved to be left to that drakking sand sucker." He looked to Rillian. "Galen informed us that the map can't be decoded."

Rillian nodded. "Unfortunately, it's missing some sort of key."

Neve made a growling sound, and Corsair brought her hand up to his lips. "We'll find her."

"Galen also informed us about the murders," Corsair added.

Rillian leaned back, placing his threaded hands on the desk. "The Thraxians are warning me off."

Neve tensed. "Will you stop helping us find Zaabha?"

"I don't cave to pressure from anyone, Ms. Haynes."

Neve blew out a breath. "I need to find my sister."

"And I need to remind the Thraxians that they were unwise to mess with me and mine. I'm planning to help Galen find Zaabha. And I will help destroy the Thraxians."

Neve went still. "You'll ensure my sister is safe before you burn Zaabha to the ground."

"Of course."

"You've had no success with the map, either?" The woman's voice was ripe with frustration.

"No."

"We've been asking around," Corsair said. "We have nothing."

Rillian steepled his fingers. "Galen has had Zhim and Ryan working on it. I've had some of my security team, some of the best on the planet, take a look. So far, we've had no luck deciphering it. They assure me that without the key, the map is worthless."

"The witch was sly, cunning," Neve said. "Hungry." She glanced at Dayna.

Dayna felt her muscles tighten. "Yes, I feel that hunger. The symbiont...requires feeding." She blew out a breath and looked at Rillian. "Which is something I'm still working on."

"So the witch is still toying with us from beyond the grave," Neve continued. "There is another piece to the map, a missing key. She wouldn't have made it impossible to find."

"So where's the rest of it?" Dayna asked. "Where is this missing piece?"

"What if it died with her?" Rillian suggested.

Corsair slid an arm around Neve. Dayna watched, fascinated, as the tough woman melted into the man's touch.

"We won't give up," Corsair said.

Neve looked up at him, a soft look on her face, and nodded.

She trusted him. Dayna blinked. They'd clearly been through a lot, if a woman as tough as Neve trusted this man so completely.

Suddenly, Dayna felt a twinge through her belly. A pang of hunger.

She shot Rillian a panicked look.

Black and silver eyes took her in and immediately understood. All smooth charm, Rillian rose. "Thanks to both of you for coming in. I'm sorry it's been a wasted trip. Rest assured, we aren't giving up, and we'll be in touch as soon as we have news."

Corsair nodded. "If I get anything from my desert contacts, I'll pass the information along."

"Please, I'd love to extend the entertainments of the Dark Nebula to you both."

The pair stilled, and then Corsair grinned. "A crowded, noisy casino full of people. Ah, maybe next time."

Clearly a casino wasn't an attractive prospect when you spent your life in the vast quietness of the desert. Dayna clenched her hands together, fighting the rising sensations inside her. She could hear the pair's solid heartbeats.

"How about a plush, private suite, including a plunge pool?" Rillian said with a faint smile.

Corsair cocked his head. "Well, that—"

Neve elbowed him. "Not today."

Corsair grinned. "Goodbye, Dayna."

Neve gave her a nod. When the woman's perceptive gaze skated over Dayna's face, she mentally urged the couple to hurry.

"Someone will meet you at the elevators to escort you out," Rillian said.

Once Corsair and Neve left, Dayna let her hands fall to her sides and pulled in some sharp breaths.

Rillian skirted his desk. "Dayna—"

The pain was growing—in her gut, her chest. It twisted hard, and God, it was horrible. She bent over, tears pricking her eyes.

A warm hand wrapped around the base of her neck. "You need to feed."

She couldn't let this keep happening. It was time to face her new reality. On her own terms.

She looked up at him. "Help me? Please, help me feed."

RILLIAN FELT a ripple of heat through his body. His symbiont stirred.

He nodded at Dayna. He saw unease in her gaze... but also trust. That was something he knew she didn't give easily.

Satisfaction flooded him. He realized he wanted this woman's trust more than anything.

He grabbed her hand, leading her toward the couch.

He sat and pulled her down beside him. She perched nervously on the edge.

He turned her hand over, studying the strong lines of it. So damn capable. Then he pressed her palm to his chest. Her fingers clenched on his shirt.

"Start small," he said. "Don't do it in an overwhelming rush. And remember, I'm giving freely."

She swallowed. "Can I hurt you?"

Always thinking of others, his Dayna. "I won't let that happen."

She blew out a breath. "Is it...? How should it feel?"

"For me?"

She nodded, pushing a strand of her hair back behind her ear.

"It isn't unpleasant," he answered diplomatically. "Every feed is different."

"And for me?"

"It isn't supposed to hurt, Dayna. How it feels is different for everyone, and every combination of people."

She licked her lips. "It hurt when the witch fed." There was a faint tremor in her voice.

That drakking bitch. Rillian wished the witch wasn't dead so he could show her just how it felt to be prey. "Because she wanted it to."

"Is it...?" Dayna's fingers flexed on his chest "...sexual?"

Ah. "Not every feed. Again, it depends on the people. A symbiont can't create attraction where there is none." He placed his hand on hers, rubbing the thundering pulse at her wrist. "Remember, the symbiont doesn't generate emotions, only amplifies what's already there."

She nodded again, setting her shoulders back. "I'm ready."

"Start when it feels right."

She closed her eyes, and a second later he felt it, a pleasant tug at his chest.

He kept his gaze fixed on her face. Her eyes snapped open and were glowing molten gold. She increased the pull of energy she was taking from him. Her lips parted. "Rillian—"

"You're doing well."

But as she fed, she shifted restlessly. And Rillian felt desire ignite in him like fire. His symbiont flared to life and his cock hardened. He gritted his teeth.

It appeared that with Dayna, feeding would be sexual.

"I'm hurting you," she gasped.

"No."

"I can see the way your jaw is tensed." Her voice was husky. "Your body's stiff."

Drak. If only she knew. "I'm fine, Dayna. Keep feeding."

She pressed closer. "I... I..."

Now, he saw something else in the glow of her eyes. *Desire. Heat.*

Control it, Rillian. He gripped his thighs, fingers digging in hard. But he couldn't stop himself from moving a fraction closer. She moved, too, their bodies brushing. Her hand was hot on his skin.

Then they were reaching for each other. She straddled one of his thighs. She was moving her hips against him, still taking energy from him.

Drak. She was the most beautiful thing he'd seen, and he could feel his control slipping.

"I'm hot." She was riding his thigh now, and reached up with her free hand to tear her shirt open. Her breasts spilled out, full and gorgeous. Her honey-gold skin was flushed and he saw the stone glowing bright gold on her chest.

His needs—all of them—were so strong. He wanted to feed on her and draw her tantalizing energy into him. He also felt a driving need to push her down on the floor, slide inside her, and fuck her brains out.

He was holding on to his control by the thinnest thread. She was riding his thigh hard now, hair tumbling around her shoulders.

"Rillian." Her voice was thick and husky. "Feed. Take from me."

He groaned. "This...is about you."

"Rillian." Her head fell back. "Feed, please."

A joint feed. A give and take.

"I want you to do it," she murmured.

That husky admission snapped his control. He could almost hear the echo of it in the room.

He reached up and yanked his shirt open, buttons flying across the floor. He crushed her close, his mouth slamming down on hers.

Instead of her palm to his chest, he pulled her closer until he felt her breasts and the hot stone below them press against his skin. Then he fed.

He pulled energy from her, driving her hips faster, feeling the heat and damp between her legs on his thigh.

His own power flooded her, and her energy raced through his body.

Light flared, and she cried out his name.

Drak. So good. She was on the verge of coming and he was about to spill in his trousers. And Rillian didn't care at all.

CHAPTER TEN

Dayna felt Rillian's energy swamp her. It was huge, deep, and powerful. A well of power that she gorged on.

And she felt him drawing from her.

She was riding his thigh faster now, each undulation rubbing against her swollen clit. Desire was so intertwined with the energy that she couldn't separate them.

He yanked her up toward him, and his mouth closed over her breast. *Oh*. His clever mouth was magic, sucking on her nipple. She looked down at his dark head pressed against her skin, and she could also see his symbiont glowing silver along his spine.

God, she was so close to coming. She moved against him again, brushing against the rock-hard cock under his trousers. She wanted to feel him inside her. She wanted to feel that powerful body taking hers.

She reached down, stroking the hard bulge covered by a thin layer of fabric. He moaned and she felt a rush of power. It had nothing to do with energy swelling between them, and everything to do with want and need.

Dayna quickly flicked open the fastening on his trousers. She slid her hand in and stroked the thick cock she found. They both groaned.

Dayna felt her orgasm growing closer. She ground down on his hard thigh, and with all the power coursing through her, she couldn't hold back.

Suddenly Rillian lifted his head. His eyes were a wicked, flickering silver. Their gazes locked, and she saw everything she felt reflected in them. Need, want, desire.

His mouth was on hers again, tongue stroking inside. She sank her hand into his silky hair, her hips moving rapidly now.

Her orgasm blindsided her. As her body shattered with pleasure, a scream was ripped from her throat. The deluge of pleasure made her body shake. She kept stroking Rillian's cock, and a second later, she felt him tense. His cock pulsed, spilling warm come over her hand, and his body shuddered.

"Dayna," A tortured groan.

They sat there for a long moment, their panting the only sound in the quiet office.

God. She licked her lips. She'd never felt anything that intense before. She was completely wired. Vibrating with pleasure and energy.

She looked up and saw Rillian's serious expression.

She sighed. "This is where you tell me that this was a mistake, and you can't take advantage of me. Blah, blah, blah."

Long fingers tangled in her hair and he tilted her head, pressing a light kiss to the side of her neck.

"This is where I tell you that you'll be in my bed tonight. And I will be inside you the next time you come." His voice lowered. "And the next time you feed, you'll also do it while riding my cock."

Her mouth dropped open, and her belly spasmed. "Oh. Well, then."

The smile he shot her was sexy and satisfied. The man was far too gorgeous.

"That's all you have to say?" he asked. "You usually have more. A lot more."

She shifted against him, loving the feel of his skin on hers. "I'm ready to tangle with you, Mr. Owns-Half-the-Planet."

He gripped her chin and pressed a quick kiss to hers. "Good. Be ready."

Heat coiled through Dayna's belly.

A second later, she heard the now-familiar chime of his communicator. They both groaned.

Rillian pulled the device from his pocket, not relinquishing his hold on Dayna. "This had better be really good."

"Rillian."

Tannon's serious tone made Dayna freeze. *Oh, no.* All the good feeling she'd been enjoying started to slide away. She knew what the man was going to say before he said it.

"There's been another murder."

Rillian's face was inscrutable, a muscle ticking in his jaw. "Where?"

"At your Dark Fire Distillery."

DAYNA CLIMBED out of the sleek transport and stared at the huge, hulking, metal-and-stone warehouse.

Rillian led the way up to the entrance, and they passed several armed security guards before they stepped inside the huge, cavernous space.

Galen was standing inside, his black cloak falling over his muscled shoulders. Raiden stood beside him, his face grim.

"Galen, you didn't have to come," Rillian said.

"You aren't alone in this fight," the imperator said. "I wanted to remind everyone of that. This isn't just an attack on you, it's an attack on all of us."

Rillian nodded. "Thank you."

Nearby, Dayna saw several loaders hovering above the ground. Rows of boxes and glass bottles were stacked against one wall of the distillery. The other side was clearly where the whiskey was made. Massive glass tanks, twice her height, were linked by snaking tubes and equipment she didn't recognize.

"We make the Dark Fire whiskey here," Rillian said. "It's one of the most sought-after drinks on the planet."

Of course, it was.

They saw Tannon's large form ahead. The man nodded, and led them down the row of large tanks. They were all filled with different-colored liquids.

As they circled one, Dayna looked at the next tank and spotted the shadow inside. There was a body floating in the clear fluid. She heard Galen mutter a curse.

They stopped nearby, staring at the dead woman floating inside. Dayna glanced at Rillian. His jaw was set like stone. He was staring hard at the woman in the tank.

Dayna catalogued the victim's appearance. She had short, dark hair that floated up in a cloud around her head. She had a small, wiry body. Most alien species on Carthago were larger than humans, but this woman looked like she would only have been an inch taller than Dayna.

"Who is she?" she asked.

"A memory."

Rillian turned to Tannon and his team. "Clear out the tanks. All of them."

Several people made choked noises.

"Sir." A distillery worker stepped forward. "Not all the tanks would have been contaminated—"

"Clear. Them. Out. Discard the whiskey."

Tannon gave one nod. "You heard the boss. Get to work." He waited until the crowd cleared. "The camera feed was jammed at the time she was dumped. They must have—"

"They probably had her do it," Rillian said. "She had a talent for that."

He turned and stalked into another row of tanks. Dayna shared a look with Tannon and Galen, then followed. Clearly this woman had been a part of Rillian's past. Someone he'd known well.

"Let me help," she said quietly.

He stopped and spun, slamming his fist into some

nearby crates in an explosion of fury. He punched a hole in the side of one box with a groan of metal.

"Who was she?" Dayna asked.

"My first lover," Rillian said. "Drak, it feels like a lifetime ago. She was a street rat like me, before she turned into a cyber thief."

Dayna had seen the hard lines on the woman's face. She'd clearly lived a tough life.

"Netta never got out," he continued. "She never wanted to. I haven't seen her in years. Drak, decades."

"Whoever the Thraxians have doing this knows you," Dayna said.

His gaze flashed. "I will stop them." He glanced back in the direction of the dead woman. "And they will regret it."

Dayna didn't doubt it. Rillian was a force of nature, especially when riled.

He shook his head before glancing at his timepiece. "It's time for the party. It's Mia's big night." Rillian reached out and took Dayna's arm.

"I don't much feel like a party," she said.

"Me, neither."

They met the others by the door.

"My team will continue working here," Rillian said. "Are you coming to the party?"

"Of course," Galen said. "Mia is excited and nervous about singing." He glanced back at the tanks. "And we could all do with a reminder that life is for living."

They were quiet on the ride back to the casino, and Rillian left her at her room. "I'll see you at the party."

"Rillian." She grabbed his arm. "You aren't alone. Don't let the anger grow."

His eyes flashed. "Are you going to help me find another way to deal with it?" He rubbed a thumb across her lips.

"Yes."

A hot look. "I'll see you soon."

Dayna showered away the feeling of death, and when she entered the bedroom, found a gorgeous dress lying on her bed.

She rubbed her palms on her drying cloth, studying the garment. It had a fitted, strapless bodice in deepest black. The long skirt was golden, and made from a fascinating, textured fabric she'd never seen before. Dropping the cloth, she pulled the gown on. She'd never worn anything like this before. The bodice molded her perfectly, and the gold skirt was fitted, but with a slit up one side that showed a lot of leg. She felt like some sort of goddess.

Rillian was good at making her feel that way.

She fumbled through her growing pile of belongings. She found a set of earrings she'd bought at the Kor Magna Markets, back when she'd first been rescued by the House of Galen, before she'd been re-snatched by the Thraxians. She remembered that day. She, Mia, and, a still-blind Winter had reveled at the chance to wander the markets. They'd giggled, bought pretty jewelry to celebrate their freedom, and had fun.

One set of her earrings had been destroyed when she'd been re-captured, but Mia had kept these this pair safe for Dayna—pretty earrings with a single teardrop stone in a glossy black. She threaded them through her earlobes.

She took a deep breath. They would stop the Thraxians, stop the murders, and they would find Zaabha and save Ever and Sam.

Through the black bodice of her dress, she fingered her symbiont stone.

Life went on for those who survived. She thought of the murdered women, whose lives had been cut too short. She thought of her fellow rescued humans, loving and living here on Carthago.

Life went on, and it was time to embrace it.

RILLIAN SCANNED THE PARTY, feeling edgy. The drinks were flowing, the servers were passing around large platters of delicacies, and the guests were smiling and laughing.

He glanced at the door. Again. He allowed himself to acknowledge the fact that he was waiting for Dayna to appear.

He spotted Galen and Magnus, deep in conversation, and moved to welcome the imperators.

"Good evening."

"Rillian," Galen said. "Nice party."

The imperator's scarred face was impassive. Rillian hid a smile. Galen didn't particularly enjoy parties, just considered them the necessary evils of running a gladiatorial house.

Nearby, the House of Galen gladiators and their

mates stood in a group. The gladiators were wearing their leathers and harnesses. The women were wearing dresses of all different colors. Mia stood beside her mate, fiddling with her short, blonde hair. Vek was picking up on her nervousness, and the blue-skinned man was making small growling sounds.

Rillian made small talk with the group, but kept checking the door for Dayna.

Finally, he spotted a tall brunette and a flash of gold.

The crowd parted, and Rillian felt his heart stop.

She was stunning.

He'd had the gown designed for her and chosen the colors to complement her coloring. She was smiling as she moved through the crowd.

Spotting their group, she headed in his direction. Rillian's gaze was on her, but he didn't fail to see men noticing her and turning to watch as she walked by.

One man was bold enough to step in front of her and smile.

Something dark flashed inside Rillian. He'd taken a step forward, hating the way she laughed at the man. Then she shook her head and pulled away.

Rillian let his curled hands flex.

"Not you, too," Galen muttered.

Rillian glanced at his friend. "They push at you and then pull you under."

"And you look like you'd happily drown," Galen said.

"I'm sorry. You asked me to protect her—"

The imperator shook his head. "I've learned that these women will protect themselves. If you're lucky, they might let you stand beside them." A faint smile edged Galen's lips. "You should know that the women have been placing bets on you and Dayna."

Rillian shook his head. He'd been alone and kept his business private so long that he wasn't used to being the subject of teasing speculation.

Magnus sipped his drink. "I don't understand the attraction of keeping a woman. They...are problematic."

Rillian skewered the cyborg with a look. "One day, you'll understand." Then turned to meet Dayna. "You take my breath away." He pulled her in for a hard kiss.

She pressed a hand to his chest, leaning back and gasping for air. "How about you just brand me, instead? Your name, right here." She touched her forehead.

"I like that idea."

She shook her head, pushing him away. "Behave."

From nearby, Galen laughed. It was almost a rusty sound.

Dayna turned to face Galen. "Any word on Zaabha?"

The imperator shook his head. "Not yet."

Rillian watched her shoulders sag.

"We need to find the missing piece of the map," Rillian said. "The witch had to have left it *somewhere*. All part of some manipulative game."

"She's taunting us." Frustration filled Dayna's voice. "Even though she's dead."

At that moment, the other Earth women called her over. With a hesitant smile, she walked over. Rillian watched as they embraced her. True friendship. These women helped and supported each other, no matter what. Mia hugged Dayna the hardest and he saw Dayna hold on tight.

"Any more evidence at the latest murder scene?" Galen asked quietly.

A muscle ticked in Rillian's jaw. "No. But the Thraxians have signed their death warrants."

He kept watching Dayna. She and Mia stood with their arms around each other. He would protect her.

The only way to do that was to find Zaabha and ensure its destruction.

CHAPTER ELEVEN

"God, tell me that man burns up the sheets," Rory said.

Dayna choked on her drink. "I'm not telling you anything."

Mia grinned. "These alien men sure know how to make a woman feel good." Her gaze moved straight to Vek. He was staring at Mia intently.

"You're truly happy?" Dayna asked.

They'd been through so much together, walked through the darkest of times. Mia had held Dayna's hand during the worst of their captivity.

Mia grabbed her hand again now. "Yes. So happy. Vek's protective to the point of driving me crazy, but he's mine. He loves me and I love him."

"And Winter?" Dayna scanned the room and found the dark-haired woman, looking like she was mid-argument with her gladiator.

"She loves keeping her gladiator on his toes, and she

loves working in Medical. Galen's purchased a bunch of different stuff for her. She's ecstatically happy."

Dayna let her gaze drift over the group of women from Earth. They were all stunning in their glittering dresses, and each one was laughing and smiling. Their overprotective gladiators stood close by, always within reach. The women were making lives here. Good ones.

"I'll always miss Earth," Mia said, as though she could read Dayna's mind. "But it's a bittersweet sting now. That said, I will *always* miss coffee. The stuff they have here isn't the same."

Dayna pulled her friend in for a hug.

Then Mia's face turned serious as she studied Dayna's features. "There is something going on between you and Rillian, isn't there?"

"We're still working it out," Dayna said.

"He's not just a suave, charming businessman," Mia said.

Dayna was fully aware that Mia hadn't actually asked a question. "No, he's not."

"I can tell he's...powerful," Mia added.

And dangerous. Dayna found him unerringly, standing in the crowd talking easily with the imperators. She licked her lips. "I like it. I like him."

"I want to ask more about how you're adjusting," Mia said awkwardly. "I'm just not sure how."

Dayna knew instantly what Mia was worried about. She gripped her friend's shoulder. "I'm adjusting to the symbiont. I haven't fully accepted it yet, but I'm working on it. And Rillian's helping me."

As if summoned by her thoughts, Rillian appeared

beside her. He touched a hand to Dayna's lower back and an electric sensation skated through her.

"Mia, the stage is all yours," he drawled.

"Oh, God." Mia ran her hand down her pretty blue dress. It shimmered under the lights. "Right. Well. This is it."

"Knock them dead," Dayna said.

Mia turned and gave Vek a quick kiss. The blue-skinned alien watched his mate intently as she took the few steps up to the stage.

"Hi, everyone, I'm Mia," she murmured.

There was no visible microphone, but Rillian had explained that they had amplification devices focused on a certain spot on stage to magnify the sound of Mia's voice.

Mia swallowed and shot everyone a smile. "I'm going to sing for you." She glanced once more at her mate before she launched into a song.

The entire room went silent, watching, entranced, as Mia sang. Her gorgeous voice rose and soared, filling the space.

"She's amazing." Dayna turned her head and watched Vek. The alien man's rugged face was transfixed.

Rillian slid an arm around Dayna, and together, they listened to Mia's song of desire, want, need, and love.

Hot lips brushed Dayna's ear. "Later, you're mine."

Dayna shivered. There was sultry promise in his voice.

Mia sang another two songs. When she finished, she was mobbed by people wanting to talk with her.

"I need to check in with the staff," Rillian said, squeezing Dayna's arm.

She shook her head. "Go do your 'I'm Boss of the Planet' thing."

His eyes narrowed. "Later, I'll show you who's boss."

She pressed her tongue to her bottom lip. "Promise?"

Rillian's gaze flashed silver, locked on her mouth. "Behave." He turned, the crowd parting for him.

Dayna looked back at Mia and smiled. Vek was standing right behind her, scowling at anyone who got too close. Dayna circled the edge of the crowd, waiting for her chance to congratulate Mia. The woman had hummed a lot during their captivity, but none of them had any reason to sing. Dayna had never guessed Mia had the voice of an angel.

"Excuse me, Dayna Caplan?"

Turning, she saw one of the black-clad servers standing nearby.

"Yes?"

"I have a message for you from Tannon," the man said.

Dayna tilted her head, wondering what was wrong. "What is it?"

"He requested your help at the security office. He was hoping you could assist him, as he didn't want to interrupt Rillian during the party."

Dayna smiled. She was finally breaking through and gaining Tannon's trust. She glanced over at Rillian. He was talking with Galen and Magnus again. He smiled, looking the most relaxed she'd seen him in a while.

This was one small thing she could take care of for him. She nodded at the server. "Thank you."

As she headed out, a slim hand grabbed her arm. She turned to see Winter.

"Hey, having a good time?"

Winter nodded and smiled. "I am. Nero hates these things." The brunette's smile widened. "I promised him extravagant sexual favors afterward."

Dayna snorted. Again, she saw a wealth of love in her friend's eyes. God, it healed something inside her to know that these two women who'd become so important to her were so happy.

"I need to help Rillian's head of security with something, but I'll be back shortly."

Winter nodded. "I'll have a drink ready for you. Don't be too long, or I'm guessing a sexy casino owner will come and find you."

Dayna was smiling as she headed out of the party. She moved toward the elevators, her high-heeled shoes clicking on the floor.

She'd find out what Tannon needed, then come back and dance with her friends, and then after the party...she shivered. Thinking about later tonight made her skin flush hot. She couldn't wait to tear that tailored suit off Rillian.

She was going to do delicious things to that man.

Dayna entered the elevator and touched the screen, keying in the floor for the security office. The car shot downward smoothly, and she watched the alien text on the panel change. She made a mental note to get Rillian to teach her the local written language. It could come in useful. Hopefully, there was some sort of simulation or implant that would speed up the process.

All of a sudden, the elevator jerked to a violent stop, with a horrible metallic screech. Dayna threw her hands out, barely stopping herself from falling to the floor.

The lights flickered, then went out, plunging her into darkness. She pressed a hand to a wall. *What the hell?*

Suddenly, red emergency lighting flooded the car.

Shit. This was all she needed. Still, she was sure the security room would see something had malfunctioned.

Then she heard a hissing sound.

Turning, she saw a strange-looking, purple gas flowing up through the cracks in the floor of the elevator.

Ah, that can't be good.

RILLIAN FELT an unsettled sensation coming from his symbiont.

He frowned at the unfamiliar feeling. He scanned the crowd, searching for a certain brunette. Where was she? His shoulders tightened.

He looked at Galen. "Have you seen Dayna?"

"Not for a while." As the imperator frowned, it tugged at the scar on his face. "Is something wrong?"

Rillian scanned the room again. "I'm not sure."

Spotting several of the Earth women nearby, he headed toward them. "Has anyone seen Dayna?"

Winter inclined her head. "I saw her before. She got a message from the head of your security team, and she went to take care of something."

Rillian stiffened. He hadn't received any message. He turned away, lifting his communicator. "Tannon, is Dayna with you?"

"No."

"Did you contact her?"

"No."

Rillian's uneasiness turned to full-blown fear. "Find her."

The noise of the security room came across the line. "I'm searching for her now."

Rillian was already striding across the party room, headed for the door. He wasn't surprised when Galen and Magnus flanked him.

"Trouble?" Magnus drawled, voice cool.

"Maybe." Rillian's symbiont was writhing now, sending panic through his veins. He never panicked.

"Rillian," Tannon said. "An elevator on the northern bank is stuck. It's showing a malfunction."

Adjusting his stride, Rillian aimed for the elevators. "Which one?"

"B13."

Rillian stopped in front of the sleek doors to elevator B13. He reached out and pressed the controls, but nothing happened.

"Sir?" The urgent tone of Tannon's voice made Rillian's blood run cold. "Scanners are showing *Zavir* in the elevator car!"

Rillian's gut cramped, and he heard Galen curse under his breath. *Zavir* was a deadly, poisonous gas.

Gripping the groove between the closed doors, he shoved to pry them open. But they only budged a fraction.

He had to get to Dayna. Pulling on his symbiont for more strength, Rillian shoved the doors open with a groan of metal. He looked down into the shaft. The car was too far below for him to even see it.

He shifted, moving one foot over the drop.

"Rillian—" Galen stepped closer.

Rillian didn't hesitate. He stepped out into the elevator shaft. His body dropped downward like a projectile.

Air rushed at him and then he saw the car appear below. He bent his legs, preparing to land.

Thump. He landed hard with a bend of his knees, his symbiont absorbing most of the impact. The metal dented beneath his feet.

Thump. Galen landed beside him in a crouch. *Thump.* Magnus landed across from them, denting the roof of the car even more.

Rillian's senses picked up a sickly-sweet trace of the *Zavir* gas.

There was no sound.

Agony ripped through him. The gas was messing with his abilities, but he couldn't sense Dayna's energy, couldn't hear a sound from inside.

Imagining her lifeless body tore him up. He'd been fighting his growing feelings for her the moment he first saw her open her eyes.

Then he heard something. A muffled thumping coming from inside the car.

Like someone was hammering on the ceiling beneath his feet.

Fear and desperation fueling him, Rillian dropped to his knees. He tore at the metal panels. He wrenched one off and tossed it into the shaft. He pulled strength from his symbiont, tearing more panels off. Galen and Magnus helped.

He couldn't lose her. He *wouldn't* lose her.

Then he saw the sheet of thick, reinforced metal that lay beneath the surface panels. *Drak.* This was taking too long.

"Watch out." Magnus' cool voice. The cyborg raised his synthetic arm, curling his fingers into a fist. As soon as Rillian and Galen leaned back, Magnus slammed down, punching through the metal.

Rillian instantly grabbed the ruined panels, ripping them open more.

Instantly, he saw Dayna's sweat-slicked face. She had her legs pressed to the walls, holding herself above the dense cloud of thickening gas.

She was alive.

He grabbed her hand and yanked her up through the hole.

Drak. Drak. Drak. His heart was pounding hard. He pulled her to his chest.

"God, I thought I was dead." Her hands twisted in his shirt.

Rillian tightened his arms around her. Below, he could see the gas billowing in the elevator car.

"It needs to be contained before it escapes," Galen said.

Rillian nodded and pulled out his communicator.

"Tannon, I've got Dayna. But we have an elevator car filled with *Zavir*."

"I'm on my way with a containment team."

Rillian looked up and saw they were close to the doors to one of the floors. He rattled off the number.

Magnus leaped across the gap, gripping the edge of the closed doors. It took the cyborg seconds to pry it open. Galen leaped across after him to help him hold the doors open.

While the imperators held the doors, Rillian lifted Dayna into his arms.

"I can make it—"

"Shh." He leaped across the gap.

They were on one of the hotel levels. The elegant corridor was empty.

Rillian dropped to his knees and buried his face in Dayna's hair. His insides were a chaotic mess. He tried to calm the fear and fury...and the burning need for revenge.

"Rillian—"

"Just be quiet and let me hold you."

She stilled, her arms tightening on him.

A moment later, another elevator dinged. The two imperators shifted, pulling their swords, and stepping in front of Rillian and Dayna.

Rillian saw Tannon step off the elevator, along with his containment team. They all wore fitted, high-tech enviro suits and helmets. Rillian jerked his head toward the shaft and his head of security nodded.

As his man directed the containment, Rillian let

himself absorb the feel of Dayna—the sound of her breaths, the solid thump of her heart. She was alive.

But Rillian was shaken to the core.

He'd amassed a fortune and built an empire. He'd vowed to never make himself vulnerable again. To never have anything in his life that could release the killer within him.

Yet here he was, with his greatest vulnerability in his arms.

Tannon reappeared, tearing the helmet off his enviro suit. "The containment is almost complete." A muscle ticked in the man's jaw. "I will personally oversee how we can avoid anyone accessing the elevators again."

Rillian nodded. Tannon was loyal as desert rock. The man would work day and night to make that happen.

"This was in the elevator." Tannon handed over a heavy piece of paper covered in writing. Rillian's mouth flattened. It was just like the others.

Your lover is dead. More will die. Forsake the House of Galen.

Rillian's rage flared white-hot like a supernova. He let out a growl and Galen took the note from his fingers.

"Rillian, calm down." Dayna rose on her knees, cupping his face.

"No." He rose, pulling her with him.

"Rillian—"

He clamped his hand on hers. He let his gaze drift over her face before looking at Galen and Magnus.

"I will burn Zaabha to the ground, and then I will grind the House of Thrax, and every Thraxian, to dust."

CHAPTER TWELVE

———————————

Dayna was trying to fight off the shock, but her close call had violent shivers wracking her body. She gritted her teeth and tried to relax in Rillian's arms.

He stepped off the elevator—that he'd had Tannon check twice before they'd used it—and onto the penthouse level. Tannon led a team of security guards behind them.

Rillian strode down the hall and past the door to her bedroom. A moment later, he carried her through the large double doors at the end of the corridor and into his room.

"No one gets in without my permission." He slammed the doors closed.

Dayna got the impression of black paint and warm woods, with a dash of blue. He set her down on the large bed covered in a glossy black cover. It felt divine under her fingers.

"My personal physician will be here shortly."

"Rillian, I'm fine—"

When he skewered her with a look, she closed her mouth. He started pacing across the large room. The lights of the city glittered through the large windows.

Dayna settled back on the bed, distractedly brushing the sleek, soft cover. A moment later, there was a soft knock at the door. Rillian opened it, and a tall, thin man with long, white hair entered, carrying a small black bag.

"She was exposed to *Zavir*. Check her."

At Rillian's curt order, she rolled her eyes.

"Hello there, young one." The physician sat beside her on the bed. "I'm Healer O'Garrie. Rillian's paying me a lot of money to check you over."

"I'm afraid he's wasting his money, I'm feeling fine."

"*Zavir* poison is not something to be trifled with." A wide smile in a friendly face. "Let's take a look."

The man pulled out a small scanner and ran it over her. He hummed, and after a few beeps from the device, he set it back in his bag. He looked at Rillian. "She's in perfect health."

Rillian gave a tight nod. "Thank you, O'Garrie."

"Get some rest." The healer patted her shoulder.

Dayna murmured her thanks, and watched the doctor leave. The door clicked closed behind him.

She lifted her chin. "Satisfied?"

"No." Rillian strode to the edge of the bed. "I want to check you myself."

Her chest hitched. "Rillian, you heard what the doctor said—"

"Strip."

A blunt command. She sucked in a breath and stared

up into his face. She saw that this was a man standing on the very edge.

She swallowed and slowly rose. Only inches separated them, and she felt the heat pouring off his body. She touched the fastenings of her gold skirt and they parted. The fabric slithered down her legs. She sat back on the bed in tiny black panties and the fitted black bodice of her gown.

Rillian pressed one knee to the bed, leaning over her. She got a hit of his spicy cologne. God, the man smelled so good.

His fingers brushed over the few inches of belly bared between her panties and top. A featherlight touch, but sensation whispered over her skin.

"When I realized you were missing..." He moved his hands, sliding them down her legs and then up again. "When Tannon told me there was *Zavir* in the elevator, I thought I'd lost you." Rillian looked at her like he was mesmerized and memorizing every inch of her. His fingers skated back up her legs, his touch turning harder as he kneaded her muscles.

She shifted on the bed, biting down on her lip. Soon her belly was filled with flickering flames.

"I thought you were gone from my life and I couldn't bear it."

Dayna stared at the beautiful lines of his handsome face. He was so gorgeous, especially with the threads of silver sparking in his black eyes. "I'm alive. I'm right here."

His fingers moved up, nudging her legs apart. He brushed her inner thighs, then teased the line of her panties. She sucked in a sharp breath, her breasts rising and falling.

His gaze moved up and lingered where the top of her breasts spilled over the top of her bodice.

"You are so beautiful, Dayna."

No one had ever called her beautiful. Athletic and attractive, but not beautiful. She needed him. She needed this man more than she needed to breathe.

She pushed up to sit, and then slid onto his lap. She tore his shirt open and leaned in, pressing against the warm, bronze skin of his chest.

Dayna felt the warm throb of her symbiont, and she knew it was enhancing the desire that was already burning hot inside her.

Rillian's hands slid down, cupping her ass, and moving her closer. Then his mouth was on hers.

She moaned, bucking against him, her tongue tangling with his. He tasted of smooth alcohol and hard man. He pushed her down on the bed and leaned over her, caging her in with his powerful body.

She stared up into his hungry face as he nudged her legs apart.

"I'm going to rip these tiny panties off you and eat you until you scream."

The dirty words said in such a charming voice made her shiver. *Oh. God.*

"Let's see how sweet you are—" he nipped at her inner thigh "—under all that sexy competence and practicality."

She gasped, writhing under his touch. He leaned

down, pulling one of her legs over his shoulder. Then with his other hand, he tore her panties off.

"Rillian."

She felt his warm breath against her folds, then one long finger slid inside her.

"Drak you're tight," he growled. "And wet."

She lifted her hips up, not sure if she would survive this. Then he lowered his dark head and his mouth was on her.

Sensations exploded, and Dayna arched up, moaning.

His tongue licked and flicked. Her hands flexed on the covers. He sucked at her, his tongue delving inside. Then he found her clit.

"Oh...don't stop," she panted.

He made a sexy growl against her, sucking her clit into his mouth.

He was relentless, not giving her a chance to catch her breath or to compose herself. He pushed and pushed, another finger sliding inside her. His mouth and fingers kept driving her higher and higher.

Without warning, her orgasm crashed over her. Dayna screamed, bucking against Rillian's mouth.

Her body shaking, she flopped back on the bed.

"I need to be inside you." Rillian pushed off the bed in a single, violent move. His suit jacket fell to the floor, and then he tore open his trousers. Finally, he stood beside the bed, naked. Gloriously naked.

Holy hell. "You know, it's so unfair to every other male specimen in the galaxy. Not only are you rich, handsome, and have a gorgeous body, you've also got the most perfect cock I've ever seen." Her gaze dropped, skating over his hard, long length.

He smiled.

Dayna felt a trickle of something deep within her, and the uniqueness gave her pause. She'd dated, and on Earth, she'd had a perfectly good sex life...but nothing or no one had ever made her feel like this. She was filled with a hungry, edgy tension, and he hadn't even been inside her yet.

Rillian gripped her ankles and yanked her toward him. She slid across the covers to the very edge of the bed. With a flick of his wrist, her bodice loosened and was gone. Then he was leaning forward, his lean hips between her legs. The intensity on his face made her belly tighten. Then he reached down, gripping her hips, and moving her exactly where he wanted her. With one hand, he circled his cock, rubbing the head of it between her folds. She moaned.

"So wet and needy." His voice was low and husky.

"Yes, I am. Inside me. Now." She moved against him, watching a smile curve his lips.

"I like it when you beg."

"Inside me now, Rillian, or I'll hurt you—"

He drove into her with one solid thrust.

"Oh!" She reached her arms out, her hands digging into the bedcovers. She was so full, she needed an anchor, something to keep her from flying apart.

Rillian started thrusting. "I want you. All of you. You'll give yourself to me."

Desire was rising inside her, insistent and raw. His

eyes were pure silver, and so hungry. She'd never been needed like this before.

"I've got you," he growled. "I'm going to take it all from you."

She saw the hunger etched on his face, but at the same time, she could feel the control he was leashing it with. His body was still tense, even as he thrust inside her.

She was right on the edge, her body trembling with the need to come again. Any second, she would go over into oblivion, but this time, she wanted him with her.

Rearing up, Dayna raked her nails over his shoulders. "I've got you, too."

With a groan, he lowered his head and kissed her. Hard, rough, and punishing. He groaned again, his body shuddering, and she felt that iron control of his slip.

"Let go," she urged.

"No."

"Yes!" She arched against him, lifting her hips to meet each one of his heavy thrusts. Their cries mingled. She was so close to coming again, but Dayna was determined to make him hers, to take him with her.

HUNGER CLAWED AT RILLIAN.

Drak. What the hell is this? He hammered into Dayna's tight body, feeling flames lick up his spine.

He pushed her back, and she arched upward, her breasts pushed forward. He ran his hand down her toned belly. Then he looked at where his cock plunged into her.

Mine. He was claiming this woman of Earth. *His.*

Her slick body clamped down on his cock. He felt another orgasm coming.

"Yes, again," he rasped. "Come again."

Her head thrashed on the covers. "I can't—"

"You can."

Her gaze met his. It was glowing gold. "Come with me."

He buried himself to the hilt inside her. She writhed, thrusting up. No sweet, submissive lover, his Dayna.

Sliding into her with long, solid strokes, more husky cries were ripped from her throat. He gritted his teeth, fighting off his orgasm.

He slid a hand down her sweat-slicked body, and found the fascinating nub of her clitoris.

Two more strokes and she screamed, her body clenching down on his cock.

"Drak!" With two more thrusts, he lost all semblance of control. His vision flashed red, and his fingers clenched on her skin. Her scream echoed around him as he poured himself inside her with a shout.

For the first time ever, he felt drained dry.

Chest heaving, Rillian collapsed beside Dayna, rolling sideways so he didn't crush her. He pulled her close.

She moved her head, her lips brushing his chest. "Well..." Her husky voice was lazy and relaxed. "The ladies were right."

He looked down at her satisfied face and arched a brow.

She smiled. "Sex with an alien rocks."

He smiled, taking her in. He'd never get tired of looking at her. All that gorgeous, sweat-slicked skin was pure temptation.

Feeling like celebrating, he pulled away and walked over to the small, built-in bar on the other side of the room. From the cooler, he pulled out a rare bottle of *Mirah*.

When he turned back, he saw Dayna was up on her side, blatantly watching his naked body.

He fought a smile. When her gaze met his, she grinned at him. No shy smiles or coy looks from Dayna. It was just pure appreciation in her eyes.

He let his gaze slide down her naked body and gave her the same back. He sauntered back to the bed and sat beside her.

"I thought we'd share a glass of this." He lifted the bottle. "*Mirah*."

"Rory tells me that it tastes almost like something we call champagne on Earth." She cocked her head. "You didn't grab any glasses."

"No need. I have a far better idea." He lifted the bottle and poured a splash down her chest.

She gasped.

Rillian lowered his head, lapping the golden liquid off her skin. *Delicious*. He licked one nipple and she moaned.

"It tastes better off your skin." He lifted the bottle to her mouth and she closed her lips around it. He tipped it, watching her throat work as she drank. Then he pulled it away, leaned forward, and kissed her gorgeous mouth.

Bubbles fizzed between them, and one of her hands tangled in his hair.

Then he pushed her back, running the bottle down between her breasts. Her eyes glowed, just as her symbiont stone did. He tipped more of the drink on her belly and lapped it from her navel.

She tilted her hips up. "Oh, God."

He spilled more of the wine over her mound, watching it slick down over her swollen folds. He lowered his head again, licking at her. Her cries were sharp and husky.

"I need you again," he growled.

Her teeth sank into her bottom lip and gold flickered through her eyes. Rillian dropped the bottle, not even bothering to watch it hit the floor and roll away. He gripped her hips and flipped her over onto her belly. She pushed her ass back against him and he shaped his hands over her glorious curves.

Then he moved in behind her, covering her body with his. "I'm rock hard again, Dayna. I can't be sweet or gentle."

She pushed back against him. "I don't want sweet or gentle."

He notched his cock between her thighs and then slammed inside her body.

"Yes!" She rocked back against him.

Again, Rillian lost his grip on his iron-hard control. He thrust into her with wild abandon, driven by an urge to possess he'd never felt before. He also felt the strangest sensation from his symbiont—like it wanted to possess as well.

This time, both their cries of release echoed off the walls as they came.

DAYNA LAY SPRAWLED on the sheets, one arm outstretched and one leg cocked.

She might never be able to walk again, and she was perfectly okay with that. She felt lips press against her bare shoulder and she smiled.

"I got you all sticky." His fingers drifted down the side of her body.

"We're both sticky," she murmured.

"Come on." Rillian's arms wrapped around her and he lifted her into his arms.

"I've never been carried as much as I have been since I came here." Dayna secretly loved it. She was tall and athletic, and carried a lot of muscle tone. On Earth, there hadn't been many men who would be able to carry her with ease.

"I like carrying you."

She'd assumed he was taking her to the bathroom, but when the glass doors to the balcony opened, she stiffened. "Rillian, we're naked!"

"Don't worry. I like my privacy, and no one—" his voice lowered "—*no one* gets to see you naked but me."

The possessive vibe to his voice made her shiver.

She swallowed. "Ryan told me that Zhim has a fancy pool out on his balcony."

Rillian made a sound close to a snort. "Zhim has a

need to be showy and flaunt his wealth. He has a pool that screams for people to look at it."

Her lips twitched. *Says the man who owns the wealthiest, classiest casino in the city.*

Hidden lighting clicked on, bathing the balcony in a soft, golden glow. She gasped. A small plunge pool was set into the floor, and protected on either side by high walls. It had a gorgeous mosaic tile bottom, and was a private little haven.

It was gorgeous. Like a magical grotto.

Gauzy, white curtains hanging from a wooden frame above the pool floated in the warm nighttime breeze. Straight ahead, she had the perfect view of the horizon, and Carthago's moons, hanging above the shadowed desert.

"It's beautiful."

Rillian stepped into the water and set her on her feet. The water lapping at her was the perfect temperature and she pushed away, ducking under. When she rose and turned back, he was leaning against the edge, watching her. Like an emperor watching his latest acquisition.

Gorgeous man. And for the moment, he was hers. His gaze was unwavering and she sucked in a breath. He *saw* her. All of her. All the good and all the bad. Everything she'd been before, and everything she was now.

He took another step into the water, and she moved closer to him. He stood only thigh-deep and her gaze dropped to his hardening cock.

On that big bed inside, he'd driven her crazy, over and over again. She'd lost count of how many times he'd made her come.

Time to drive him wild.

She dropped to her knees on the bottom step in front of him. He paused, cocking his head.

"Time for me to have some fun." She pressed her hands to his hard thighs.

"Fun?"

"Yes." Anticipation licked her belly.

"You want to suck my cock, Dayna?"

Her fingers dug into his hard muscles and the water lapped at her breasts like a caress. Her gaze locked with his. "Oh, yes."

"And I want to see your lips wrapped around me." His fingers cupped her jaw. "I want you to suck me until I come in your mouth."

Dayna's belly clenched. She licked her lips and leaned forward. She ran her tongue over his magnificent, long cock.

He made a noise and it spurred her on. She took him in her mouth, enjoying the salty taste of him. She sucked him deeper.

Fingers stroked her cheek and his hips moved minutely. He was still exerting that fierce control of his.

She adjusted her angle and took him deeper. His groans urged her on, and a sense of power filled her. His fingers tightened on her jaw, and having this powerful, dangerous man under her spell was intoxicating.

"Hold still, Dayna." His words were raw, ripped from him. "I'm going to fuck that sexy mouth now."

She obeyed, letting him direct her mouth. He started moving his hips, thrusting deeply between her lips. *God.*

"Can't last...much longer." His face was drawn tight, a dull flush along his cheekbones.

Seconds later, he came with a groan, his hands tangling in her hair. Dayna swallowed it down.

"Drak, you slay a man." His thumb brushing her lips.

She was trembling with need again, her symbiont burning in her chest.

Rillian took another step down into the water, and swept her up against him. As he shifted, she saw his symbiont glowing brightly against his back. She reached over his shoulder and stroked it.

He stilled, turning a little. She leaned over and pressed a kiss to his back. Then he reached out, his hand caressing the stone between her breasts, and she moaned at the sensation.

His cock was hard again, pushing against her belly. As he pulled her up, she wrapped her legs around his hips.

"Need you," he growled. "Can't wait."

She didn't want him to wait. He thrust inside her.

Dayna's head dropped back, her fingers digging into his shoulders. As that thick cock worked in and out of her body, she felt a violent need to feed rising up inside her.

She tried not to panic, but she couldn't control it, couldn't stop it.

"Rillian." She heard the fear in her voice.

"Take what I freely give, Dayna."

She leaned into him, their chests slicked together. Then she released her fierce hold on herself and felt the energy pull from him into her.

It felt so good. Like being drowned in a wave of pleasure. "Feed from me, too," she panted. "While you're deep inside me."

He made a feral sound and didn't pause in hammering into her body. A second later, she felt the reciprocal flow of energy as he pulled it from her.

Her eyes widened. Gold met silver. The pleasure was unlike anything she'd felt before.

Her orgasm blindsided her. It was almost like an explosion, energy flowing over them as pleasure burst through her. As she screamed his name, she heard his harsh roar as he came.

And then, for the first time in her life, Dayna blacked out from pleasure.

CHAPTER THIRTEEN

R illian held Dayna's limp body in his arms, trying to regain some control. *Drakking stars.*

She'd brought him to his knees. He dropped down to sit on one of the pool steps and gently pulled her into his lap, stroking her back.

Her eyelids fluttered and she curled into him in a very un-Dayna-like way. She murmured something unintelligible, and he smiled. He very much liked wearing Dayna Caplan out.

He stroked a hand down her spine and she turned more to give him better access.

Then he paused.

Golden markings glowed at the base of her neck, spreading out across her skin. They were alien symbols.

He thumbed them, his body tense.

"What?" She looked over her shoulder, moving lazily against him.

"There are alien markings on your skin. Beneath the skin, I should say."

She sat up. "What?"

"They're glowing the same color as your symbiont." That drakking witch. Rillian really wished she was still alive so he could kill her himself.

Dayna pushed her hair forward over her shoulder. "What do they say?"

He stroked the wet silk of her hair and thumbed the markings. "Drak." It couldn't be.

She wriggled. "What?"

"Dayna, I think these are the missing piece of the Zaabha map."

"Seriously?" She looked at him over her shoulder, her eyes wide.

"I think the witch inscribed the last piece of the map on your skin." He lifted her, and with water streaming off both of them, carried her inside. Setting her by the bed, he strode into his large walk-in wardrobe. He found his black robe and grabbed another for Dayna. After slipping his on, he moved to her and felt a spurt of annoyance at having to cover up that lovely body. It was too big, but she belted it and folded the sleeves up.

"Sit on the bed and loosen the robe a little."

She complied, and he grabbed his communicator. He pushed the robe off enough that he could take clear pictures of the markings. Then he tugged the silky fabric back over her golden skin.

He showed her the screen and her gaze narrowed. She fingered the markings on the image.

"They're almost pretty," she said. "If they didn't possibly lead to a hellish arena."

Rillian tapped the screen, accessing the data he had on the stone map that Neve and Corsair had recovered from the witch.

"Let's see if these symbols piece together with the other map." He set his program to run, images whizzing quickly over the screen.

No match.

He released a breath. "They don't fit."

"Maybe the tattoos are something else." Dayna frowned, wrapping her arms around herself.

Rillian swiped his screen, putting through a call.

A second later, an angry face appeared on the screen. "This had better be life or death."

Zhim, Carthago's premier information merchant, had an impressive scowl. His dark hair tumbled around his shoulders and he was shirtless.

Ryan's head popped in from the side and she rolled her eyes. Her black hair was pulled back in a messy bun. It looked like the Earth woman was wearing Zhim's shirt. The blue fabric swamped her tiny body

"Ignore him," Ryan said. "He means, 'hello, it must be important. How can we help?'"

Zhim crossed his arms. "No, I don't."

"Hang on a sec," Ryan said.

Rillian waited, hearing rustling from off screen. Ryan returned, her hair a little tidier and wearing a smaller shirt. It had something written on it.

If you break it, I'll fix it, but it will cost you.

Rillian swallowed a grin. He couldn't have found a better match for Zhim.

"Hi, Ryan," Dayna said quietly.

"Dayna. Hope you're okay?" The woman's dark eyes took in Dayna and Rillian's matching robes and she grinned.

A faint flush filled Dayna's cheeks. "I'm...fine."

"We are sorry to interrupt," Rillian said. "But we discovered something that could be important." He told the pair about Dayna's tattoos.

Zhim's scowl morphed into a look of concentration, his nebula-colored eyes glowing. There was nothing Zhim liked more than getting his hands on new information.

Both geniuses turned to the comp screens behind them and started tapping.

"Can you send the images through?" Zhim asked.

"I already have," Rillian replied.

"Got them." Ryan made a few small humming noises and Zhim leaned over his lover's shoulder.

Rillian picked up Dayna's hand and squeezed. "I tried to see if the markings slotted in with the map, but got nowhere."

"It'll be encrypted," Ryan said. "I'm running some of our decryption algorithms."

Zhim nodded, his fingers flying over the screen. "Enhancing now."

As Rillian watched the pair, he realized how well matched they were. The small, intelligent woman from Earth, and the wealthy, arrogant information merchant. Zhim glanced down at Ryan, and the woman winked at him. There was a smile on Zhim's lips, and while he hadn't softened exactly, he seemed less harsh than he had been before. Happier.

"Got it." Ryan pumped a fist into the air.

On the screen, Rillian watched the map shimmer, and the alien markings off Dayna's skin slide around and fit into it.

"Overlaying on aerial images of the desert," Zhim said.

Rillian now saw a glowing blue dot marked deep in the desert west of Kor Magna.

"It's in the Plain of Burning Sands," Zhim said. "Horrible place."

Rillian had never been there, but he'd heard the terrible stories of the endless heat, and sand so hot it melted anything that touched it.

"Tell Galen," Rillian said. "I'll have my pilots prepare my desert ship." Minerals in the desert sand didn't mix well with ship engines. Most travel in the desert was confined to simple vehicles or beasts. The more complex the engine, the more the sand clogged it up. "We'll leave first thing in the morning."

"Rillian," Zhim's voice was grim. "I have scans of this area from two weeks ago. There was nothing there."

Dayna leaned forward. "There must be *something*. We have to find it. We have to save Ever and Sam."

Zhim gave a single nod. "I'll tell Galen to prepare to leave in the morning. Good luck."

DAYNA FIDGETED IN HER SEAT, staring out at the endless yellow sand they were flying over. Rillian sat beside her, expertly piloting the ship. She watched his long-fingered hands move easily over the controls.

Was there anything the man couldn't do?

Her gaze drifted over that face that she could look at all day. She was falling for Rillian. She let out a breath, warmth filling her belly. She was falling for a sexy, dangerous man who never let anyone get too close.

Well, watch out, Mr. Gazillionaire, because I'm pretty stubborn when I want something.

Murmurs from behind them caught her ear, and she glanced back. The atmosphere in the ship was tense. Galen, several of his gladiators, Magnus, and Corsair and Neve were seated in the passenger area. The elegant ship hadn't been designed with massive shoulders and huge bodies in mind, so it was a tight fit.

When Dayna looked back out of the front window, the only thing out there was hot, baking desert. Memories shimmered and bile rose in her throat. She swallowed, and thought of Ever and Sam instead. She hoped the pair were holding on. Dayna knew the horrors of Zaabha, and she wanted nothing more than to free the women. *Hold on a little longer.*

But there was something else Dayna wanted. *Revenge.*

She patted the laser pistol holstered at her hip and the sheathed knife she'd borrowed from Rillian's weapons collection. She'd been a cop most of her adult life. She knew revenge wasn't right or polite or nice. But in this situation, she didn't care. The Thraxians and Zaabha were going down.

"Approaching the coordinates," Rillian said.

Dayna stared ahead, clenching her hands on the arms of her seat. She squinted against the bright sunlight, but there was nothing. Just sand, sand, and more sand.

Her gut clenched. "I can't see anything."

"I don't, either," Rillian said grimly.

Maybe this was a wild-goose chase. Dayna drummed her fingers on the armrest. Maybe the witch was messing with them from beyond the grave.

Neve appeared at Dayna's shoulder, leaning forward. A muscle worked in the woman's taut jaw. "There's nothing here."

"We'll find her." Dayna gripped Neve's arm. "You're not alone in this. We won't stop until we find your sister and Sam."

Neve looked down, her unique green eyes pale against her darker skin. She nodded.

"We're here," Rillian said. "Landing now."

He set the ship down, and when the ramp opened, a wave of baking-hot air filled the ship. The gladiators stood, and Galen was the first out of the door, Neve close behind him.

"Here." Rillian wound a length of beige cloth around Dayna's neck and head. "It's made from a high-tech fabric that reflects the sunlight." He'd already put his on, looking like some sexy desert sheikh.

"Thanks."

His thumb brushed her cheek, then he turned and

ducked outside. She followed and blinked against the sunlight.

"The sand here is high in a certain mineral that absorbs more heat," Rillian said. "That's how the Plain of Burning Sands got its name. Be careful."

Nodding, she scanned their surroundings. Low dunes and more scalding sand. No wild desert arena, no trapped fighters, no bloodthirsty spectators.

"There's nothing here." Despair gripped her chest. Dayna closed her eyes and memories of imprisonment assailed her. Cages, screams, the cheers. And the witch's laugh as she'd fed on Dayna's energy.

"Dayna?"

Rillian's cool voice broke the spell. She was free. She was making the choices in her life now. "I'm okay. Let's look around."

As she moved across the sand, she glanced up at the hot suns blaring down on them. Ahead, she saw Neve angrily kick sand into the air. Corsair was there, wrapping an arm around his woman and pulling her close.

Dayna fisted a hand and pressed it against the symbiont stone between her breasts. Maybe the women were dead. Maybe all the Zaabha prisoners were dead. Maybe there was nothing left to find.

A hand rested on her nape and squeezed. She leaned into Rillian, absorbing his strength. She so rarely leaned on anyone, but with him…it felt good.

"Zaabha has been hidden for years," he said. "It was never going to be easy to find."

Galen appeared. "We *will* find it. There must be something here."

Dayna looked around again. Sometimes on her cases, it was the smallest thing that had led to a breakthrough. The thing most people overlooked.

"Fan out and search for anything," Galen said. "No matter how inconsequential."

With a nod, Raiden turned, his red cloak flapping in the desert breeze. The other gladiators followed him, and he ordered them into a search pattern.

Dayna walked with Rillian, searching the sand. Then he lifted his head, glancing off toward the west, his gaze narrowed.

She paused. "What?" She looked around. "What did you see?"

"Nothing." He frowned. "I didn't see anything, but for a second, I felt something."

Felt something? Dayna looked around again. She felt the hot wind and the heat radiating off the sand. "I don't feel anything."

His eyes flashed silver. "I'm not sure what it is, but my symbiont senses something."

CHAPTER FOURTEEN

Something tickled along Rillian's senses. He turned in a slow circle, and Dayna glanced at him, then back at the sand. She was studying the ground intently. He knew her previous employers on Earth must miss her skills and focus.

"I don't sense anything," she said, huffing out a breath.

"Use your symbiont's enhanced senses," he told her. "Embrace them."

She nodded, closing her eyes. Rillian turned, blocking out the energy of the nearby gladiators. There was another hum of energy coming from somewhere.

She opened her eyes and shook her head. Frustration was stamped on her face.

"Don't push so hard." He gripped the back of her neck and squeezed.

He spotted something in the sand nearby and walked over. He crouched down to study it. Under a thin layer of sand, deep grooves were cut into the bedrock.

"Something was here." Dayna crouched beside him. When she touched the ground, she pulled her hand back with a hiss. "Damn, that's hot."

She lifted her head, looking off into the distance. Then she jumped up.

"Dayna?"

She broke into a jog and Rillian followed. She stopped by another matching set of deep grooves in the ground.

They both stood there for a moment, frowning. The marks didn't appear to be random. They were deep, and cut into hard, desert rock. That would have required a lot of force.

"What could have done this?" she said.

He shook his head. "And what were they for?"

They walked in several widening circles, studying the sand around them. Rillian glanced over at the gladiators, and caught Galen's gaze. The imperator shook his head once before turning back to his gladiators.

Another prickle of energy whispered over Rillian's skin.

He stopped and closed his eyes. He focused on the feel of the wind brushing against his skin, and the hot sunlight hitting him. He sensed Dayna go still, but her energy was like a bright, fresh blast that he absorbed.

Then he felt the wave of unfamiliar energy again—jagged, discordant.

Then he realized what he was sensing.

It was energy from living beings. A lot of them. It was

the same as when he walked the casino floor—lots of different energy levels, from lots of different species.

He spun to look at Dayna. "What do you sense?"

She looked away from the gouges on the ground and set her shoulders back. She closed her eyes.

Drak, he loved seeing her embracing her symbiont. The cool look of control and power on her face made him proud as hell.

"I can feel the House of Galen gladiators. They put off a lot of power. Neve and Corsair." She opened her eyes, staring at the others in the distance. "Not much from Magnus."

Rillian nodded. "He can dampen his bio-signature. What else?"

"Energy." A frown tugged at her lips. "Different kinds of energy." She tilted her head. "It's distant, like a low hum."

Exactly what he was sensing. "Energy from what?"

She turned, scanning around them. "People. A lot of people."

"So where are they?" he asked, frowning.

"That's the question. There's no one here."

Oh, they were here. They just had to find them. He signaled Galen and they started walking toward the others.

Suddenly, a dark form dropped from the sky and landed in front of them with a spray of sand.

Rillian jerked to a stop, slamming an arm out to stop Dayna. A huge Thraxian rose from a crouch, and slid a sword off his back.

Another Thraxian landed close to Dayna. The alien

swung his arm, and his fist caught Dayna in the face. The blow sent her crashing to the sand.

Filled with ice-cold anger, Rillian moved. He slammed a kick into the Thraxian's gut. The man doubled over with a grunt, and Rillian followed through with a hard chop to the back of the Thraxian's large head. He slammed to the sand.

Moving on instinct, Rillian ducked. A huge, clawed hand swept over him. He spun and thrust up with an uppercut. His attacker staggered backward.

As he raced to Dayna, he heard shouts and the clash of metal on metal. More Thraxians were raining from the sky, and charging toward Galen and the gladiators.

Rillian stopped beside Dayna. She was sitting up, shaking her head. He grabbed her arm and yanked her up. Three more Thraxians landed from nowhere, surrounding them.

Yanking his knife from his belt, Rillian felt the familiar hilt settle in his hand. Dayna pulled her laser pistol off her hip and held it up. He knew she'd been practicing with it in his weapons room.

A big Thraxian stepped forward. His eyes glowed a deep orange, like burning flames.

"You should have heeded our warnings," he said, in a deep, guttural voice. "Now you will die."

DAYNA FIRED, the laser pistol whining in her hand.

One big Thraxian went down with a roar. She kept shooting, spinning to fire at the other attackers.

A huge body came in from the side and slammed into her. They crashed to the sand and her pistol flew out of her hand.

She rolled and caught a glimpse of Rillian fighting another Thraxian. God, he was so swift. He moved impossibly fast. She watched him jump, spin, then slam a fist into the Thraxian's face. The alien staggered back, and Rillian landed, and advanced.

Taking advantage of her distractedness, her Thraxian elbowed her in the gut, and the air rushed out of her. They rolled across the sand, and the alien got to his feet. She struggled to get up and he grabbed the back of her shirt, dragging her through the hot sand. *Bastard.* He was bigger and stronger.

Anger poured through her. *No. Not anymore.* These were the aliens who had stolen innocent humans from Fortuna Station. Who had destroyed the space station and killed so many. Who'd subjected innocent people to so much.

She felt her symbiont stir, feeding on her emotions. She pulled on the inner power, took a breath, and spun. She slammed her fist into his gut.

The Thraxian flew backward as though fired from a canon. The comical surprise on the alien's face almost made her laugh. Dayna leaped to her feet and strode toward the alien. She stopped to snatch up her pistol.

She reached him, set her boot in his gut, then aimed her weapon at his chest and fired.

He flopped back on the sand and didn't move. She turned and saw two large Thraxians fighting Rillian. He ducked a swing and kicked out. He took down one

Thraxian, while the other one charged him. A blow to the back drove him to the ground.

No, you fucking don't. Dayna raised her pistol, striding forward. She pulled the trigger.

Laser fire hit the Thraxian and he shuddered under the impact.

Rillian sprang upward and grabbed the Thraxian from behind. With a quick move, he broke the alien's neck. He released the body and it fell to the sand.

She ran to Rillian, her chest heaving. He touched her cheek briefly, before they both turned. In the distance, the gladiators were locked in a deadly fight with a large group of armed Thraxians, and several Srinar as well.

Jesus. Swords clashed, and Thorin roared as he swung his huge axe down. Corsair stood to the side, firing a deadly-looking crossbow.

"Come on." She broke into a run. "We need to help them!"

She and Rillian moved fast, sprinting toward the fight. Suddenly, she heard a *thwap* sound in the air.

Rillian stumbled and jerked to a stop.

Dayna skidded on the sand and turned. A huge spear had pierced his shoulder from behind. The wicked point protruding through his shirt made her stomach turn.

"No!" she cried.

His face contorted with agony, blood sliding down to soak his shirt.

She ran to him and instantly realized that it wasn't a spear. It was a harpoon. There was a length of metal cable attached to the harpoon, leading up into the air.

She grabbed onto him. "Rillian—"

Eyes the color of gunmetal met hers. Then suddenly, he was yanked upward off his feet.

Dayna reacted on instinct. She clamped her arms and legs around him. He groaned in pain, and the sound stabbed through her.

They flew up through the air frighteningly fast. *What the fuck?*

Holding onto Rillian tightly, Dayna arched her head back. Above, she spotted a giant, dark shimmer in the sky.

Her chest locked tight, her eyes widening. There was a giant, invisible, floating fortress hanging above the desert sands.

They were pulled closer to the massive craft, and she saw the bottom platform was a smoke-blackened, industrial level. Smoke churned out of exhaust pipes, and she saw what reminded her of coal-fired engines. Rillian had said fancy engines didn't work well in the desert. Grimy-faced workers looked out through the metallic bars with dead eyes, watching as they whipped past.

And then they were jerked up over a huge wall. Rillian groaned again, the agony of the sound making her heart hurt. Then, everything became a fierce blur, as they tumbled and slammed hard into more sand.

IN A WHIRL OF COLOR, sound, and pain, Rillian sprawled on the ground. Agony radiated through him from the wound on his shoulder. It felt like he was on fire.

His clothes were soaked with blood, but thankfully, he felt his symbiont compensating for the blood loss, and attempting to heal the wound. It would be sand-sucking bad if he healed up around the harpoon, though.

He managed to get to his knees, blinking away dizziness.

"Take it easy."

Dayna came into focus in front of him. She had bunched up her head covering and was pressing it to his shoulder. He saw the worry on her face. She pressed harder to staunch the blood loss and he groaned.

"Sorry." Her eyes were full of misery.

"Fine. Healing."

Something flashed in her eyes. She moved behind him, and without any warning, she gripped the harpoon and yanked it out. Hot pain flared.

Rillian shouted and fell forward.

"I'm sorry. I'm so sorry, baby." She pressed the wadded fabric against both sides of his wound.

He gripped her hand. "Thank you." His voice was hoarse.

She blew out a breath. "I hate hurting you. Now, we just have to work out what the hell is going on, and get out of here."

Now that his dizziness was easing, he lifted his head. He went still and felt Dayna do the same.

"Fucking hell," she murmured.

They were kneeling in the center of an arena.

The arena floor was covered in sand and ringed by empty stands constructed of a jarring mix of metal, wood, and whatever had been scavenged to build them. He felt the faint vibration of the engines beneath their feet.

Rillian turned his head, taking it all in. "No wonder we hadn't been able to find Zaabha."

Zaabha was on an airborne platform. It could fly, move, and stay hidden. Drakking crudspawn Thraxians.

"They must have regular set down locations," she said. "Hence, the maps. But they can go anywhere."

Nearby, a rattling sound echoed across the arena. Several large gates were clanking upward.

"This isn't going to be good," Dayna said, her voice tense.

"No, it isn't. Help me up."

They stood together as the gates stopped and stared at the dark shadows. A number of animals slunk out of the darkness. They were big and deformed, and no species of animal he knew.

"What are they?" she asked.

"I see features of hunting cats, but I've never seen a species this big." Some of the animals were severely deformed—bones twisted and large growths in strange places. "I think these are probably the result of some illegal breeding program."

"Nice," she muttered.

Another large alien creature lumbered in behind the cats. It had gray-green bumpy skin, overdeveloped muscles, and powerful arms.

He dragged in a deep breath. "That's a *larg*. Banned from the Kor Magna arena. They enjoy crushing their prey to death."

"Oh good, the more the merrier." Dayna moved in front of him and shifted into a fighting stance.

Rillian fought off a smile. Of course, she was going to protect him.

Behind the animals, he saw several fighters of different alien species move into the arena. They all wore threadbare, tattered clothes and scarred leathers. Their weapons were a haphazard mix of homemade swords and scavenged spears and axes.

These were the imprisoned fighters of Zaabha. People who had been fighting to survive for who knew how long. People that knew they had to kill or be killed.

"I don't think we're supposed to make it out of here," Dayna said quietly.

He reached out and grabbed her hand. "The Thraxians still don't understand Earth women."

She shot him a sideways smile. "Or suave casino owners who own half the planet."

She lifted her knife and Rillian pulled out his own blade.

"Let's fight." Rillian grabbed her for a hard kiss. "Don't get hurt or I'll be very unhappy."

The cats bounded in fast.

Rillian leaped in front of Dayna and, as the lead cat jumped, he timed his move, then grabbed the cat out of the air. He spun its huge bulk and threw it to the side. Dayna ran and slid in low, feet first. She slashed out with her blade. As she cut into the hide of a cat, it screeched.

Another cat flew at Rillian in a flurry of sharp claws. He dodged, and it flew overhead.

When he spun around, it was to face the bulky *larg*. It slammed a giant foot down into the sand, making the floor vibrate. Rillian raced toward the alien. He was fast and it was slow.

The *larg* swung clumsily and Rillian leaped up, jumping over the creature's arm. It was slow, but he knew that if it got a hit in, it would break bones. His shoulder screamed in pain, but he blocked it out, slashing out with his knife. He nicked the creature's cheek and it roared.

Rillian landed on the *larg's* arm. He jumped again, aiming straight for the alien's face. He rammed his blade into the soft spot between the creature's black eyes.

It shuddered, arms waving through the air. As it collapsed, Rillian leaped off, landing beside Dayna with a roll.

"Rillian."

She was tense, braced to fight, and her knife clutched in her hand.

He raised his head and saw the first wave of fighters were racing at them. He straightened, seeing the desperation and despair on their faces.

Dayna stepped forward, waving her arms. "We can get you out of here!"

The closest fighter darted forward, giving no indication he'd heard her words. He swung a rusty sword at her and she ducked, going in low to stab him in the thigh.

More fighters swarmed over them. Rillian spun, ducked, and kicked. He jumped high, slamming brutal kicks into one man's face. He landed and rammed his hand forward, taking down a tall woman. He spun, grabbed two fighters, and rammed their heads together with a crack. Both fighters dropped instantly.

Turning, he saw Dayna fighting. Drak, she was amazing. Strength and skill. Power and beauty. He watched her spin, kick, and follow through with a hard punch. Like him, she was trying not to kill the fighters.

But more were coming.

His symbiont flared, heat moving through his blood. He was going to get Dayna out of here.

Whatever he had to do to ensure she lived, he'd do it.

As he pulled more power from his symbiont, he knew his eyes would be a brilliant flashing silver. He lifted his head and the attacker rushing at him hesitated, his battered sandals kicking up sand.

Rillian smiled and spread his arms, ready to fight. Whatever it took, he would save Dayna.

CHAPTER FIFTEEN

S weat was dripping into Dayna's eyes. She swung out with her knife, then ducked and weaved through the fighters.

There were just so many of them...and they all looked like they had nothing left to lose.

Something whacked into her side from behind. With a grunt, she went crashing to the sand. She spun and looked up at a giant, green-skinned alien fighter with a staff.

The staff slammed down again and she rolled. She moved to jump to her feet, but the alien leaped on her.

His heavy weight drove her into the sand. She smelled unwashed body and turned her head.

"Look, we're here to shut this place down. We can get you out." Bracing against the smell, she looked up...into dead, blank eyes.

He pressed his staff against her throat. Wrapping her hands around the rough wood, she tried to keep him from choking her. She saw that the man had some sort of metal implant embedded at his temple.

Dayna pulled power from her symbiont and sent the man flying off her. He grunted, spun in the air, and landed in the sand.

She leaped to her feet, power surging through her.

For the first time since her rescue, she felt like she and her symbiont were one. And it felt good.

Searching for Rillian, she spotted him fighting a tall man. Two big aliens were moving in on him from behind. She raced toward him.

She watched him toss one fighter away. One of the big aliens rushed at him, slashing at him with a sword.

That's when she saw the other big fighter circling around, holding a large spear. Her chest went tight. The first fighter was toying with him, keeping him busy.

"Rillian!"

At her shout, he lifted his head...just as the second fighter thrust the spear into his side.

"No!" she cried.

She watched Rillian drop to his knees. He clutched the spear protruding through his gut. Dayna sprinted harder. He'd already lost so much blood from the harpoon, but now she watched more red flow down his side.

But he was still fighting.

He reached up and jerked one opponent to the ground. He drove the man's head into the ground. The second fighter's eyes widened and he took a step back. Rillian rose, then yanked the spear from his gut.

Dayna stumbled to a stop nearby, wincing. The pain had to be excruciating.

Rillian turned and lifted the bloodstained weapon. He strode toward the fighter, who spun, ready to flee.

With a powerful toss, Rillian speared the man through his shoulder. The alien fell to the ground. The blow was hard enough to pin him to the sand.

She reached him. "Rillian."

"I'm okay." His face was sheened with sweat. "Keep fighting."

They turned, and she saw more fighters racing out of the open tunnel. An athletic woman led the charge, moving quickly across the sand.

Dayna stiffened. The woman was almost as tall as Dayna, with dark, matted hair, skin shades darker than Dayna's, and pale green eyes. "Oh no."

She'd seen the woman's picture before and she looked a lot like her sister. It was Ever Haynes.

The brunette showed no recognition. As she reached them, she swung a rough, jagged sword. Dayna leaped back, dodging the blade. She got a close-up view of the silver implant protruding from Ever's left temple.

"Ever? Ever Haynes."

No response. The woman lunged forward, swinging her sword again.

Dammit. Dayna rolled across the sand. She didn't want to hurt the woman.

Ever turned away from Dayna and attacked Rillian. He bent backwards fluidly, the sword passing within an inch of his face. But Dayna saw him clutch his stomach wound and wince.

Gritting her teeth, she charged forward. She leaped on Ever, taking her down to the ground. The woman struggled, but her face stayed strangely emotionless.

What did they do to you? As Ever tried to buck her off, Dayna gripped the woman's head. "I'm sorry."

She slammed the woman's head against the ground. Something flickered in Ever's eyes before they closed. She was out cold.

Chest heaving, Dayna got to her feet. She glanced over and saw Rillian limping toward her, dragging one leg behind him. He was leaving a trail of blood on the sand. Her heart clenched.

Fighting back her fear for him, she reached down and gripped the neckline of Ever's tattered shirt. She dragged the woman with her as she and Rillian moved back toward the center of the arena.

Fighters were circling them, but they were wary now.

"I'll distract them." Rillian pulled in a breath, his eyes like quicksilver. "You climb into the stands and find a way off this thing."

Dayna shook her head wildly.

"I want you off this." His tone was autocratic and commanding.

"No." She shook her head again. "I know you're planning to sacrifice yourself for me. Not going to happen, Rillian. For once, you'll have to deal with the fact that I'm someone who won't follow your orders, and someone who cares about you."

He reached out, fisting her shirt with one hand. "Live, Dayna. You have to live."

She lifted her chin, emotions storming through her. "Without you, I wouldn't be living, I'd be existing."

He muttered a vicious curse and yanked her in for a quick kiss. "Drakking hell, I'm falling in love with you."

"Well, I'm falling in love with you, too." Her throat was tight, her symbiont stone flaring. This amazing man was hers.

But first, they had to survive.

As they turned, she saw more incoming fighters had entered the arena. Her pulse spiked. So many. Too many.

Dayna stiffened her spine. She wasn't damn well giving up now. She had always fought to protect, and she would do it again now.

She'd fight, with the man she was falling in love with by her side.

RILLIAN FELT the blood dripping out of him, his energy draining away.

But he had to keep his woman alive.

The fighters rushed closer, and he knew he wouldn't be able to stay on his feet for long.

He pulled in a breath, looking at Dayna as she stood over the unconscious Ever. Dayna was tensed and ready to fight. He realized now that she would always fight for what was right.

And he would always fight for her.

There was only one thing he could do to ensure she lived. The one thing he'd fought his entire life to control.

Rillian let his arms fall to his sides. "Dayna, whatever

happens, stay back."

Her eyes widened. "Rillian."

"Stay back and stay alive."

He relinquished all control, letting his symbiont free. Energy flooded through him in a wave, and washed all the pain away.

His vision turned acute and hunger swamped him. Emotions washed away leaving him with the need to hunt and kill. Feed and thrive.

Win. Whatever the cost.

He crouched down and snatched up a fallen sword. As the fighters rushed at them, Rillian leaped into the air, spinning and swinging the sword around.

He cut through opponent after opponent.

He grabbed the closest fighter and the man struggled against him. Rillian pressed his hand to the man's chest.

Energy filled him and he smiled. The man's body shriveled and turned to dust. He grabbed another enemy and fed. Another.

As rich, potent energy sang through him, he turned to see more fighters were coming. A never-ending supply of energy. His symbiont pulsed—hungry and wanting.

He plowed through another wave of fighters. He fed, he killed, he fought.

When he rose from the littered bodies, he saw the fighters were hanging back. Watching him with fearful eyes.

"Rillian!"

Through the roar of energy, the voice penetrated. It sounded vaguely familiar.

He turned and saw a tall, brown-haired woman

taking down a fighter. She was a fierce fighter and filled with pure, untainted energy.

He tilted his head. He knew her.

Dayna. It was like a whisper in his soul. *Dayna.*

Mine. His. Rillian's.

Suddenly, a giant alien charged at her with a wild cry.

Heat seared along Rillian's spine and his symbiont relinquished its control. "Dayna!"

The alien swung a huge fist, and Dayna's body flew through the air. She hit the sand, rolling over and over. She stopped on her stomach. She tried to push herself up, but fell back down.

Rillian fought his way toward her, swinging the sword with wild slashes. He didn't care who got in his way, he would make it to her.

He got closer and saw she was crawling, pulling her bleeding body across the sand. She was hurt.

A giant shadow fell over her, and a clawed hand sank into her hair. The alien yanked her up viciously, holding her dangling above the sand. Her face was clenched in pain.

Rillian paused. It was a Thraxian. Both his horns had been broken off and his orange eyes leveled on Rillian. "Rillian."

Recognition flickered. Old memories of his years running scams resurfaced. "Vral."

He hadn't seen the Thraxian for years. The man had run some jobs with Rillian...until Rillian caught him stealing from him and cut him out.

"I was hired to send you a warning not to mess with

Zaabha," Vral growled.

Cool fury ignited. "You killed those people."

An ugly smile. "You always pretended not to care, but I knew you did. Always so arrogant, thinking you were better than the rest of us."

"I still am," Rillian said.

Anger flashed in Vral's eyes. "You stole from me. Left me with *nothing*."

"You stole from me, and broke our agreement."

Vral took a step closer. "I've spent *years* dreaming of getting my revenge."

Rillian tilted his head. "And I haven't given you one thought."

Something ugly flickered in Vral's eyes. "Now I have your woman." He shook Dayna like a doll.

Rillian shook his head sadly.

Vral cocked his head, his brows drawing together. "You're bleeding out and will die on this sand. And I have what's yours and I will hurt her!"

"No, you don't have her." Rillian's gaze met Dayna's golden one. "And she's going to hurt you."

Dayna spun in Vral's grip and jammed her knife into the Thraxian's neck, working the blade through the alien's tough skin.

With a roar, Vral staggered back, but Dayna twisted, using her weight to drive them to the ground. She landed on Vral's chest, the light from her symbiont flashing through her shirt. She lifted the knife and stabbed again.

Rillian knew she was getting her revenge for everything the Thraxians had done to her and her friends. For the murder victims Vral had killed. He knelt beside her.

"Do it," she said.

Rillian pressed his hand to Vral's chest and fed.

Vral screamed and a second later, his body disintegrated.

Once again, his symbiont wanted control. Rillian fought it.

Dayna cupped his cheek and instantly, his symbiont went quiet. Dayna, what he felt for her, helped him control the alien inside him.

"You are dangerous, sexy, and I love that," she said. "All of it. All of you."

Drak, he was past falling. He loved this woman with every fiber of his being.

Then Rillian heard running steps and saw another wave of fighters rushing out of the tunnel. He muttered a curse and turned to face them.

"Dayna."

She grimly pushed to her feet and moved to his side. She was swaying a little, but lifted her blood-stained knife. "My symbiont has patched me up a bit. I can fight. Nice day for a fight."

Rillian shook his head. "I love you."

"I want to hear you say that while we're naked on your big, soft bed. So let's get this done."

They both rushed forward to meet the fighters.

Rillian spun and slashed, again letting his symbiont free. For the first time in his life, he and his symbiont were in perfect sync.

Dayna was right beside him, kicking, and swinging her knife. They smashed through several opponents.

The pain had reached levels that his symbiont could

no longer block, but Rillian kept fighting, riding the agony. It was all worth it to keep her safe.

But more fighters kept coming. The ground was littered with the dead and groaning, and Rillian knew that he and Dayna were at the limits of even their symbionts' strength.

Dayna swung out clumsily, then swayed, and went down on her knees. His own strength waning, he dropped down beside her.

"Rillian." Her voice was weak.

He lifted his head and watched the fighters coming closer, sensing their prey was weak.

"Shh, I have you." He wrapped an arm around her. If this was how it ended, they'd end it together.

"I don't want to die." She leaned her head against him. "I want to live. I want you."

"You have me, wherever we are. In this life or the next, I will always find you."

The wild cries of the fighters got louder, and her hands gripped him tightly. Rillian closed his eyes and absorbed the feel of her.

All of a sudden, there was an explosion of sound.

Rillian's eyes sprang open. He watched as the stands off to the left exploded outward. A sleek silver ship—his ship—came crashing into the arena.

Dayna gasped. The starship hit the sand, sliding through it, and plowing into several fighters.

Then Rillian watched as it kept moving wildly through the sand...rushing toward them.

Drak. It was going to crash into them. He curled his body around Dayna's and braced himself.

CHAPTER SIXTEEN

G od, their own ship was about to kill them.

Nausea from the pain clamped down on Dayna. She tightened her hold on Rillian, watching over his broad shoulder as the ship raced closer with a spray of sand.

Then, the ship slowed and stopped just two meters away from them.

Air rushed out of her lungs. *Jesus, talk about close calls.* She looked up and through the cockpit window, she caught a glimpse of Galen and Magnus at the controls.

A second later, the side door of the craft opened, and gladiators poured out.

"For honor and freedom!" the House of Galen gladiators yelled.

"Looks like we're going to make it after all," Rillian said.

She nodded, heart in her throat, as Raiden and Harper raced together across the sand. The pair leaped into the oncoming fighters. Harper jumped incredibly high, her head held up and her swords swinging.

She landed beside her man, and together they moved in a dance of hard, brutal moves. They were a solid unit, protecting each other and fighting together like they'd been doing it all their lives.

Next, came Blaine and Saff. The couple let out a wild battle cry, both of them smiling grimly. Thorin thundered after them, hefting his axe, and Kace was beside him, swinging his staff.

There was a blur of blue and Vek leaped out of the ship. He paused, threw his arms out, and let out a roar before charging in to fight.

Neve and Corsair brought up the rear, Neve's staff whirling and Corsair's electroblade glowing brightly.

"Incredible." Dayna watched the gladiators race into the fighting crowd. Galen's gladiators worked hard to subdue the fighters without killing them. Everyone knew that these people were prisoners.

She looked at Rillian. "Come on, we need to get to the ship."

A faint smile. "I can't seem to get my legs to work."

Her stomach went hard. God, there was so much blood. When she looked at his back, she saw his symbiont was glowing weakly through his shredded shirt.

"Don't worry, my symbiont is healing me." He cupped her cheek. "Just give me a minute."

Suddenly, Galen and Magnus appeared. Strong arms —one of them which felt like cool metal—helped her to her feet. She gave Magnus a nod.

Galen helped Rillian up, one arm wrapped around

his back. As the imperator took in Rillian's condition, his scarred face turned grimmer. "Looks like you should stick to casinos."

Rillian managed a hoarse laugh. When Galen shifted, Rillian stiffened. "If you try to carry me, I'll hurt you."

"Then quit being lazy," Galen said.

Rillian nodded. "I think I can move a bit now." His gaze moved to the ship as they limped slowly across the sand. "Looks like you should stick to arena fights and not flying."

Galen grunted. "Blame Magnus."

"Wait!" Dayna turned her head, searching the arena. "Ever. We found Ever." God, was she okay? "She was under the control of some sort of implant. I had to knock her out. There!" Dayna pointed to the body slumped on the sand some distance away.

Magnus gave a single nod. "Can you walk? I'll get her."

Dayna set her shoulders back and nodded. When Magnus released her arm, thankfully her knees held. She moved to Rillian's other side.

"Galen!" Raiden's shout. "More fighters incoming."

Galen cursed and Dayna saw more gates opening around the walls of the Zaabha arena. Fresh fighters were running out, shouting wildly. Her gut cramped.

"We need to go. *Now*." Galen broke into a jog, taking most of Rillian's weight.

"Is my ship still operational?" Rillian asked.

"It should be." Galen's icy gaze skated down Rillian's body. "Can you fly it?"

"Yes." A single, uncompromising word. "I want Dayna out of here."

But Dayna saw the lines of strain on his face. He needed a healer and some rest.

"What about Zaabha?" Rillian said.

"And we haven't found Sam," Dayna added.

"We'll come back," Galen said darkly. "We know what Zaabha is now. They can't hide from us."

The new wave of fighters was pushing the gladiators back toward the ship. The deafening clash of swords, staffs, and axes rang out across the sand.

Dayna looked up and saw they were almost at the ship. They were just meters away, when Rillian's legs went out from under him.

"Rillian," Dayna cried.

Galen abruptly hefted Rillian back to his feet and dragged him onto the ship. Dayna thundered up the ramp right behind them, ignoring her own aches and pains. As she reached the top, the ground started to shake and she stumbled. *What the hell?*

She looked back down the ramp, as several robots began ducking out from under the tunnel entrances. These weren't the sleek, well-maintained machines she knew the gladiators fought in the Kor Magna Arena. These were robots pieced together with hunks of metal and scrap. They belched smoke, and were covered in sharp spikes, wire, and armor plating.

The first giant robot walked closer, and with each step, the ground shook

"Drak!" Galen urged Rillian into the cockpit. "Fire up the engines. We need to go. Now."

"Come on." Dayna moved to the other side of Rillian, helping him down into the pilot's seat. "Let's get home."

Silver eyes met hers. "Home?"

"Yes." She smiled. "Our home."

Rillian's eyes flashed and he smiled back. "Then let's go."

Magnus

MAGNUS' internal heads-up display streamed with text. It warned him of the number, size, and power of the incoming enemies.

He didn't panic. He couldn't panic. He had emotional dampeners that kept him cool and focused. With a simple command, he could compartmentalize any emotions he might feel. Generally, he left his dampeners running all the time.

Life was far more efficient without emotions.

He strode towards the body of the Earth woman. A fighter charged at him with a wild, desperate cry. Magnus simply smacked the man with his cybernetic arm and sent him flying.

Another fighter leaped in front of him, swinging a ragged sword made of scrap metal. He lifted the sword above his head, and thrust it toward Magnus.

Magnus' cybernetic hand flashed out and he caught the blade in his palm. There was no way the dull sword could penetrate his high-tech metallic skin. As comprehension dawned, the fighter's eyes opened in shock. With his organic arm, Magnus slammed a hard punch into the man's face. He collapsed in the sand.

Finally, Magnus reached the woman.

He crouched, ready to pick her up, and suddenly she rolled, throwing sand into his eyes. It had no effect on his artificial eye, but his right eye stung a little. He blocked the pain.

The woman was already launching her attack, her arm swinging in a practiced move.

He caught her fist in his and finally looked at her face.

No. It couldn't be. He *knew* this woman.

Shock penetrated through his dampeners. She shifted, bringing her knee up. He deflected the blow and yanked her in close. He catalogued her appearance in a second. Tall, fit, more muscular than her sister. She wore loose-fitting leather armor. Black hair with a slight curl, and eyes the same pale green as her sibling. Although those eyes were currently dull, and under the influence of the silver implant at her temple.

Attractive.

Magnus frowned internally. He was cataloging facts, not constructing a personal opinion about what Ever Haynes looked like. His program must have a glitch.

How did he know her? He was sure he'd only ever seen her picture before. But with her pressed against his body, something whispered through him. A memory. A bone-deep knowledge of her he shouldn't have.

She shoved against him, and this time, he lifted her off the ground. She made a snarling sound, then slammed her head forward and headbutted him.

Drak. Pain flared.

He dropped her, and took a step back. She came at him again, and he gripped her arms. They scuffled across the sand, and he fought hard to subdue her without hurting her. She was very well-trained.

His gaze moved to the implant embedded at her temple. His systems scanned it, and he knew he needed to short-circuit it to release her from its control.

He touched the implant and shot an electrical impulse through it.

She let out a cry and collapsed. Magnus lowered her to the ground, and this time, when she turned her head, he saw pain-filled eyes.

"You." Her voice was low and husky.

"You know me?" he asked, frowning.

"Yes..." Her eyes fluttered, and then her face contorted.

Something was wrong. A red warning flashed on his controls. Her heart rate was decreasing.

Drak. He touched the implant again and her vitals evened out. The Thraxians had tied the implant to her main systems. Magnus cursed again. And he'd just fried it. Without it, she'd die.

His jaw hardened, unfamiliar emotions churning inside him. He had an expert medical team that dealt with cyborg implants. They would find a way to remove it.

"Can't...breathe." She tore at the armor on her chest.

Magnus helped her remove it.

She heaved in a breath. "Help me."

"I will, Ever. Your sister's here. We're getting you out of here."

"Neve." Her face went pale and she grabbed his organic hand. She pressed it to her abdomen. "Please, help me."

Magnus went still. Her stomach was swollen and rounded. It had been hidden beneath the armor. His sensors picked up a second, faint heartbeat inside her.

"Please, help the baby."

Ever Haynes was pregnant.

The words echoed in him. Magnus was unable to procreate and had never given any thought to children. But now that faint heartbeat whispered through him, along with a strange sense of awareness.

The primitive need to protect her slammed into him. Monitoring her implant and vitals, he scooped her carefully into his arms. Whatever had happened to her, he was going to ensure she was safe...and that no one ever harmed her or her child again.

RILLIAN'S VISION WAVERED, and he fought to clamp down on the pain shooting through his body.

He knew his symbiont was protecting him from the brunt of it...but with the level of pain he was still feeling, it meant his injuries were bad. He moved his hands over the controls, ignoring the blood he smeared all over them.

The engines ignited and the ship vibrated.

He scanned the screens. Thankfully, Galen and Magnus hadn't done too much damage to his ship. He ran through the checks and his jaw tightened. The engines were running close to critical from the desert sand. They needed maintenance as soon they got back to Kor Magna.

If they got back.

"Oh, God." Dayna leaned forward, her tone urgent.

He glanced through the cockpit windshield. The robots were headed across the arena, their mechanical gazes locked on the ship.

The Thraxians really didn't want them to leave.

She leaned forward more. "Can you see Magnus? Did he get Ever?" She gasped. "Oh, no."

Rillian followed her gaze...and saw Ever attacking the cyborg. Magnus dodged her hits, trying not to hurt her.

Boom. Something hit the ship and sent it rocking. Dayna fell into Rillian's lap and pain shot through him.

"Sorry!" She jumped up. "Dammit, one of those robots threw something at us."

"We need to go." He glanced out of the windshield. Galen and his gladiators were in full retreat, sprinting back to the ship. *Faster, Galen.*

Vek bounded aboard, followed by Neve and Corsair.

"Any sign of my sister?" Neve asked.

Dayna nodded. "We found her. Um, Magnus is getting her."

The other gladiators boarded, moving to take their seats.

Come on, Magnus. Rillian revved up the engines. The robots were getting closer.

"Do you have weapons on this thing?" Dayna asked.

"Yes, but I can't risk firing here. I'm likely to take the whole of Zaabha down." And kill all the prisoners.

"Dammit," she muttered.

The cyborg imperator thundered up the ramp holding an unconscious Ever in his arms.

"Ever!" Neve leaped toward her sister. "Is she okay?"

"She's alive," Magnus said in a cool voice. "But I'm keeping her alive. She has some sort of implant and its malfunctioning."

"Oh, God." Dayna's eyes were wide, resting on Ever's form.

Rillian looked and hissed out a sharp breath. Ever Haynes was clearly pregnant.

Neve made a strangled sound, her hands curling into fists. She stared at her sister's rounded belly.

"We need to go," Rillian called out.

"Strap in with her, Magnus." Galen appeared. "Everyone's aboard. We have to take off."

Movement outside the windshield caught Rillian's eye and he grabbed Dayna. "Watch out!"

One of the robots swung out with a huge fist. It slammed into the ship and sent them skidding sideways through the sand.

There were cries and curses from the back, but Rillian blocked it out. All he could focus on was the ship. One engine had failed, and he worked the controls, trying to get it started again.

"Thraxians," Dayna said, her voice tight.

He lifted his head and saw a wall of them, all armed. They were moving in formation across the sand.

Rillian worked feverishly trying to get the engine going.

"Rillian?" Galen asked.

"Working as fast as I can. I need a couple of minutes."

Galen strode to the door, pulling out his sword. "I'll buy us some time."

Raiden moved to join his friend and imperator.

Galen shook his head. "Stay here." He looked past his champion to Harper. "You have more to lose than me."

"Galen—"

"That was an order, Raiden." The imperator leaped out of the ship.

Rillian thumbed some controls, watching the system spool up. Ninety seconds. That was all he needed.

"Look at him," Dayna breathed.

Galen cut a swath through the fighters. He moved with power and skill, and a lot of grace for such a big, muscular man.

Rillian had never seen Galen fight in the arena, but people still talked about the imperator's fighting days with awe.

"There are too many of them." Dayna pressed her palms to the console, staring at Galen.

She was right. Even with Galen's skills, he couldn't keep the entire crowd of fighters and the robots away from them.

He saw Galen run through the legs of one robot, dodging its stomping feet. He raced out, circling a second robot. The two machines crashed into each other and fell over.

"Yes!" Thorin yelled from the back.

Then the Zaabha fighters started to pull back. Rillian frowned. *What were they doing?* They formed a loose circle around Galen, and started chanting, some pumping their fists into the air.

"Champ-ion! Champ-ion!"

The crowd parted and a woman strode out.

Rillian stilled. She wore fitted leather armor with blue accents, and leather boots that came up past her knees. Her muscular thighs were bare, except for the armored skirt that draped down to mid-thigh.

She was carrying a sword, and she swung it in a flashy vertical circle. She moved with a fluid grace and power that said she was fully at ease with her body. Had honed it to be a weapon.

The woman's brown hair was streaked gold by the desert sun, and pulled back from her bold-featured face. Her skin was also tinted gold. Her expressionless gaze took in the ship, before moving back to zero in on Galen.

"My God." Harper pushed forward, her voice full of shock. "The captain."

Blaine was at her shoulder. "Samantha," the man breathed.

The final abducted woman from Earth. Rillian stared. Samantha Santos was the Champion of Zaabha.

She came to a stop, facing Galen across the sand.

Suddenly, she raced forward with a burst of speed. Galen strode forward to meet her. Their swords clashed together, and they stood there, frozen, turning in a slow circle.

Rillian saw the woman say something. Galen inclined his head.

"Anyone read lips?" Blaine asked.

Dayna and Harper shook their heads.

"Let's hope she didn't say 'Prepare to have your guts spilled everywhere.'" Harper looked worried. "Sam is a hell of a fighter."

"So is Galen," Blaine countered.

With a brilliant burst of speed, Sam spun away from Galen and ran. She leaped into the air, flying higher than even Harper did in battle. She sailed over the heads of several fighters, and then...attacked the robots.

A second later, Galen was with her. The pair worked together, swords slashing. They whirled and spun, blades hacking through metal. They chopped through the ankle of one robot, and it started to topple over.

Dayna gasped. "I'm guessing they made an alliance."

Galen and Sam turned, shoulder to shoulder, swords raised.

The Zaabha fighters milled around, confused. Their champion had turned on them. Sam shouted and swung her sword, driving them away from the ship.

Suddenly, the engine flared to life and Rillian let out a breath. "Okay, we're ready to go."

He babied the ship, lifting it off the ground.

Raiden leaned out of the open door. "Galen!"

The imperator was heading back toward the ship and shouting at Sam to follow him. She moved in behind him, but at that moment, the wall of Thraxians broke into a run, rushing at them.

Sam's gaze met Galen's for a brief second, then she waved at him. She veered off and spun, facing the incoming Thraxians.

Galen cursed. His face contorted as he shouted at her.

"Now!" Rillian yelled. The longer they took, the greater the risk the ship would fail before they reached the city. Or he finally lost too much blood and passed out.

"Galen. Now!" Raiden shouted.

The imperator's mouth moved in what looked like a string of curses and he ran for the ship. As he neared, he jumped and landed inside.

He strode into the cabin, face grimmer than usual. "Get us back to Kor Magna."

Harper pushed forward. "Sam—"

The imperator's icy eye flashed, his hands balling into fists. "The fool sacrificed her chance to escape so we could get out of here. Let's honor her for that." He dropped into a seat. "And the sooner we get home, the sooner we can come back for her."

CHAPTER SEVENTEEN

Dayna stood in the stone-lined corridor outside of Medical, in the House of Galen, waiting with the others. Neve was pacing so hard that Dayna kept waiting for a groove to appear in the stone floor.

"The healers will help her," Regan said to Neve quietly. "And Magnus is helping to keep her alive."

Neve turned, her lips trembling before she firmed them. "She's pregnant. Someone hurt her!"

Dayna watched Corsair wrap his arms around his woman.

Dayna clasped her hands together. Her belly was fluttering, waiting for Rillian to be finished with the healers. She'd already had her own injuries treated, and she'd stayed with him until Galen's Hermia healers had assured her that he was going to be okay.

Still, after everything, she wouldn't quite believe it until she saw him herself.

Nearby, Harper and Blaine sat on low stools. The

two human gladiators were tense, and she knew they were thinking of Sam.

Suddenly, the doors opened, and she caught a glimpse of Magnus standing beside Ever's bed, before Rillian stepped out into the hall.

Relief filled Dayna and she walked straight to him. He looked his usual self, his skin bronze again, a faint smile on his lips. Except for his borrowed clothes. She hid a smile. She was certain the simple pants and shirt were not up to Rillian's stylish standards.

She wrapped her arms around him and dropped her head against his chest. As his arms closed around her, she slid one hand under his shirt. She stroked the smooth skin beside his symbiont, and felt a pulse of warmth. Something tight inside her relaxed.

He leaned down and pressed his face to her hair. "Dayna."

She lifted her face. "You're okay?"

"Fully healed, and my symbiont is functioning in top form." He lifted his hand, brushing his knuckles over her cheekbone. "You?"

"I'm fine, better now that I can see you're okay."

"Always thinking of others."

The doors whispered open again and Winter stepped out.

"How is she?" Neve demanded.

"She woke up for a bit." The doctor clutched her hands together, a pained look on her face. "The implant embedded in her temple extends deep into her brain. Right now, it's requiring regular electrical impulses from Magnus to keep it functioning and to keep Ever alive."

God. Dayna leaned into Rillian. *Poor Ever*.

Neve closed her eyes. "Can you remove it?"

"I'm not sure yet," Winter said. "We'll need to analyze it, and this isn't an area of expertise for the Hermia healers."

"But it is for my healers."

Dayna looked up. Magnus had stepped out of the room. He looked tall and imposing, his face like granite.

"Your healers can remove it safely?" Neve asked.

A single nod. "It will take time. She'll need to stay at the House of Rone."

Winter was studiously avoiding looking at the cyborg. "There's...more."

"The baby," Neve whispered. "Is...is it Thraxian?"

Winter cleared her throat. "No. The baby is a genetic mix of several species, including human."

"She was experimented on?" Angry color flushed Neve's face.

"Ah, no. But the father is a genetically-engineered mix." Winter twisted her hands together.

"Wait." Corsair kept a tight arm on Neve. "You know who the father is?"

Magnus shifted. "I'm the father."

Silence reigned for the span of a few heartbeats, then chaos exploded in the narrow hallway. Voices rose in confusion and surprise. Neve slipped out of Corsair's grasp and lunged at Magnus, slamming a punch into his gut before Corsair dragged her back.

"Oh, my God," Dayna murmured.

Rillian's arm flexed. "This is...an unexpected development."

Galen stepped into the bedlam. "Enough."

Silence.

Neve glared at the cyborg, her gaze shooting daggers.

"I don't have answers for you, yet." Magnus' face was impassive. "I was imprisoned in the desert for several days a month ago. It appears I met your sister in that time."

"You don't remember?" Neve's voice rose, her eyes sparking.

"My memory was impaired during my rescue. And I have certain programming that means I cannot procreate." A muscle ticked in the imperator's jaw. "So, I don't have all the answers for you yet, but—" his voice lowered "—I can vow that I will find those answers, and I will protect your sister and that child with my life, with all the resources of the House of Rone, and everything that I am."

Neve vibrated with tension for a long moment, then she sagged weakly against Corsair and nodded.

"Everyone get some rest." Galen stepped forward. "We'll meet again for dinner to celebrate Ever's rescue." His icy gaze met Dayna and Rillian's. "I've organized a room for you. Once you've rested, please join us for dinner. We couldn't have found Zaabha or Ever without your help."

As the crowd dispersed, Rillian kept his arm around Dayna, and they followed a House of Galen worker to their room. Her old room. She hadn't stayed in it long before she'd been snatched again, but walking inside, she saw they'd kept it just as she'd left it.

The airy room was dominated by a large bed covered

in fur rugs. A well-appointed bathroom contained a huge bathtub.

Rillian opened his mouth to speak, but Dayna moved to him, tearing his shirt off. She pressed her palms to his skin—over his shoulder, his stomach. Over where his wounds had been.

"Dayna—"

She shook her head, nudging him back to sit on the bed. "I need to see that you're okay. I need to feel it." Her voice caught. "I need to hear your heart beating."

He went still under her touch. She stroked him all over, loving his quiet groans and the heat building in his eyes.

She stepped back, sliding out of the simple clothes she'd pulled on after she'd showered in Medical. Naked, she climbed onto his lap, pulling his face to hers. Their kiss was long and slow.

But it didn't stay that way. Need grew and turned molten. She undulated against him, feeling his hard cock beneath her. One of his clever hands slid between her legs.

"Do you need me here, Dayna? Deep inside you?"

"Yes."

It took him seconds to free his hard cock. Then with his help, she lifted her hips and slid down, taking that thickness inside her.

She moaned and started to ride.

"Just like that." He gripped her hips, pushing her down to meet his thrusts. "I love you, Dayna."

"I love you, too." She gripped his shoulders, staring into his beautiful silver eyes.

Heat built. He surged deeper inside her, and her husky cries echoed off the walls. Pleasure slammed into her like a hard, silk-covered fist. She arched back, trusting Rillian to hold her, anchor her. Another circle of her hips, and she felt him drive deep, holding her there as he ground his cock inside her and came hard.

He pressed his head against her breasts. "Be mine. Now. Always."

She sank her hands into his silky hair. "I feel like I've been waiting for you all my life, and I never knew it."

Kissing her chest, he fell back on the bed, pulling her with him. He wrapped around her and Dayna sighed, feeling a sense of contentment she'd never experienced before.

His fingers slid up her belly, one hand cupping a breast while the other caressed her symbiont stone. "How's your symbiont?"

"I think it's happy. Content."

"Good," he said.

She stroked his back, her fingers brushing over his symbiont. "And yours?"

His eyes flashed and he pushed her onto her back. "I think it's feeling hungry again."

"You seem...more accepting of it."

He paused. "It's content too, Dayna. I unleashed it when I had to, but thinking of you, seeing you, it helped me rein it back in."

She smiled. "See, having someone close isn't a scary thing."

He nipped her lips, his cock prodding between her legs. "Only if that person is you."

RILLIAN SAT at the large dining table in the gladiators living area, talking with Galen.

"How's Ever?" Rillian asked.

Galen lifted his drink. "Awake and doing fine. Magnus is with her."

Rillian's gaze drifted to Neve...who didn't appear to be having a very good time. "The baby was unexpected."

Galen raised a brow. "For Magnus, most of all. She'll move to the House of Rone tomorrow. The first priority is removing her implant."

Across the table, the women were trying to be happy, but Rillian picked up on the somber mood in the room. Everyone was excruciatingly aware that one human was still missing.

"So, Zaabha can move wherever the Thraxians want to move it," Rillian said.

Galen nodded. "It explains how it's remained a secret so long. The guests—"

"The scum," Raiden said from the other side of Galen.

The imperator nodded. "The spectators receive an invite to a location in the desert that changes every time. From the brief amount that Ever has shared, it only sets down for the fights and to take on supplies."

"I'm assuming that it's moved from the location where we encountered it."

Galen stared into his glass. "Yes, Ryan and Zhim have confirmed that. But—"

"But?"

A flash of an ice-blue eye. "I don't care. We know what it is now and I will find it again. I will *not* leave Samantha Santos there." Galen's hand tightened on his glass. "And I will destroy Zaabha and the Thraxians."

"Whatever I can do to help, you only have to ask."

"Thank you, Rillian."

A burst of laughter made them both look up. Rillian watched Dayna laughing with Regan and Rory, and something settled inside him. A heat that warmed his soul washed over him. He hadn't even realized how cold he'd been before. His controlled, empty life had been missing one very important thing.

"Something tells me the lovely Dayna won't be returning to the House of Galen," Galen said, his voice desert-dry.

"You can't keep them all, Galen."

Dayna spotted Rillian looking her way and shot him a saucy wink.

"This one is mine." Her body, her heart, her soul.

"She looks happy," Galen said.

"I'll enjoy keeping her that way."

"Oh, my God." Rory suddenly stood, cradling her giant belly.

From beside Rillian, Kace shot to his feet, his gaze on his wife. In a swift move, he leaped over the table, setting glasses and plates rattling. He jumped down beside Rory.

"Rory?"

The redhead's eyes were wide. "I...I think the baby's coming."

Rillian froze and saw the gladiators do the same. The

looks ranged from happiness to terror. Nothing like a baby to panic a group of huge, muscled fighters.

Dayna rose, completely calm and collected. "Okay, Regan and Winter, let's get Rory and Kace down to Medical."

The women leaped into action.

"You're going to have a baby," Winter said.

Kace swept Rory off her feet. "Let's move."

Dayna smiled, ushering the group out. As she touched Rory's shoulder, her body bent close to Rory's, Rillian had the perfect image of Dayna's belly, swollen with a child. *His* child.

He smiled, taking a sip of his drink.

One day. Rillian was a man who always got what he wanted.

DAYNA LEANED AGAINST RILLIAN, once again standing outside Medical. Waiting really sucked, and everyone was tense and tired.

Dinner had ended hours ago, and everyone had been listening to Rory's screaming and cursing echoing through the corridors of the House of Galen. She'd called Kace some pretty colorful names, sworn off sex, and threatened to murder her husband if he came near her again.

Nero had already vowed to never impregnate Winter, and the other mated gladiators were all looking a little pale.

The last time that Kace had come out to update

them, the brave, military-trained gladiator had been white-faced.

Nearby, Raiden was pacing, while Regan and Madeline were playing some sort of card game. It had been quiet for a while, and Dayna wondered what was happening behind the doors.

Rillian's arm tightened. "Do you feel it?"

She stilled, opening her senses. *There.* She smiled. A bright, new burst of energy. "You have to teach me more of what my symbiont is capable of."

"It'll be my pleasure."

All of a sudden, the doors opened, and Kace stepped out. He held a tiny bundle in the crook of his arm.

He was beaming. "I have a son!"

Cheers erupted, and the women surrounded him.

"How's Rory?"

"Can we see her?"

"Let's see the little cutie!"

Dayna watched everyone study the baby. She could hardly believe it. A half-human baby born here. After everything they'd all been through, all the terrible moments since their abduction, Dayna had never, ever imagined anything like this. That a new life would be born from the darkness.

Her eyes roamed over the women, all of them smiling and happy. Then she took in the handsome gladiators standing beside them, protectors who would give their lives for these humans.

Love and new life. Out of the ashes of their terror, something beautiful had been born.

"What's his name?" someone asked.

ANNA HACKETT

Kace frowned. "Rory and I haven't decided yet."

"That's code for they can't agree on a name," Regan said with a smile.

"Go." Rillian nudged Dayna forward. "I know you want to see him."

She joined the others, and saw that Regan had pried the baby off Kace. She was cooing to the little bundle, and the baby was looking up at them curiously with wide, green eyes.

The gladiators were all slapping Kace on the back and offering congratulations.

"Hello, little cousin," Regan murmured.

"He's gorgeous. And so alert," Madeline said. "My Jack slept for the first two days."

"He's a spitting image of Kace," Harper said.

"But he has Rory's eyes," Regan said with a smile

Saff leaned in, a curious look on the female gladiator's face. "He's very small."

"Actually, he's pretty big for a human newborn," Winter said. "And they grow fast, Saff."

Mia pushed forward, a dreamy look on her face. "I want lots of these." She cast a glance back at Vek. He was standing beside her with his arms crossed. He made a growling sound, and Mia poked her tongue out at him.

"So, are you planning some of these with Mr. Sexy Casino Man?" Harper asked Dayna.

Warmth spread through Dayna's chest. "Right now, I'm just thinking about hot sex."

Regan giggled and pressed her lips to the baby's head. "Don't listen to Auntie Dayna."

"One day," Dayna said with a smile. "I'd never really

thought about kids before. I was so focused on my career. Right now, I think I'll just practice how to make them a lot."

Saff raised her brows. "I do not blame you. That man is liquid." She winked. "And an invaluable ally, of course."

"Of course." Dayna smiled, but then a heaviness filled her. "But we still have to shut down Zaabha." She hated to dampen the happiness of the baby's arrival. But as she looked down at Kace and Rory's baby, it firmed her resolve. If nothing else, they needed to rid the world of this evil, and make it a better place for this child.

"We'll do it," Harper said with a nod.

"We'll rescue Sam," Blaine added.

Dayna nodded. "And we'll show the Thraxians once and for all that they messed with the wrong species."

Soon, Kace reclaimed his son, and the women were allowed to visit Rory.

A strong arm slid around Dayna's shoulders and she breathed in Rillian's scent.

"A new life." Rillian glanced at the baby, safely nestled against his father's broad chest.

Dayna nodded. "I love you."

"I know," he drawled. "How about we head home? I bet Chef Derol has a special meal prepared for you."

"Always trying to feed me."

"Be prepared for a lifetime of me spoiling you."

She tapped a finger against her lips. "I think I could get used to that. There is one thing I want."

"Anything."

Dayna took a deep breath. "I'd like to join your security team. I have skills they could utilize—"

"Done."

She tilted her head. "Tannon isn't going to be happy."

"The man is never happy, but I think you've grown on him."

"Like mold." She grinned. "No getting rid of me now."

Rillian pulled her closer, his palm resting over her symbiont stone...and her heart. "Never. You're mine, Dayna Katherine Caplan. Everything I have is yours, and I will protect and love you to the end of my days."

With a happy laugh, Dayna pressed her lips to his, her hand sliding up his back to stroke his symbiont. "And you're mine. I'll ignore your orders, push you when you need it, chase off all the women who dare to touch you, and love you. Always."

"Best deal I ever made," he murmured.

I hope you enjoyed Rillian and Dayna's story!

Galactic Gladiators will continue with CYBORG, the story of the cyborg imperator of the House of Rone, Magnus, and human survivor, Ever. Coming in April 2018.

For more action-packed romance, read on for a preview of the first chapter of *Marcus,* the first book in my best-selling Hell Squad series.

Don't miss out! For updates about new releases, action romance info, free books, and other fun stuff, sign up for my VIP mailing list and get your *free box set* containing three action-packed romances.

Click here to get started: www.annahackettbooks.com

FREE BOX SET DOWNLOAD

JOIN THE ACTION-PACKED ADVENTURE!

READY FOR ANOTHER?

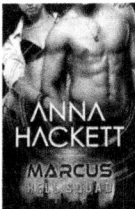

**IN THE AFTERMATH OF
AN ALIEN INVASION:**

**HEROES WILL RISE...
WHEN THEY HAVE
SOMEONE TO LIVE FOR**

Her team was under attack.

Elle Milton pressed her fingers to her small earpiece. "Squad Six, you have seven more raptors inbound from the east." Her other hand gripped the edge of her comp screen, showing the enhanced drone feed.

She watched, her belly tight, as seven glowing red dots converged on the blue ones huddled together in the burned-out ruin of an office building in downtown

Sydney. Each blue dot was a squad member and one of them was their leader.

"Marcus? Do you copy?" Elle fought to keep her voice calm. No way she'd let them hear her alarm.

"Roger that, Elle." Marcus' gravelly voice filled her ear. Along with the roar of laser fire. "We see them."

She sagged back in her chair. This was the worst part. Just sitting there knowing that Marcus and the others were fighting for their lives. In the six months she'd been comms officer for the squad, she'd worked hard to learn the ropes. But there were days she wished she was out there, aiming a gun and taking out as many alien raptors as she could.

You're not a soldier, Ellianna. No, she was a useless party-girl-turned-survivor. She watched as a red dot disappeared off the screen, then another, and another. She finally drew a breath. Marcus and his team were the experienced soldiers. She'd just be a big fat liability in the field.

But she was a damn good comms officer.

Just then, a new cluster of red dots appeared near the team. She tapped the screen, took a measurement. "Marcus! More raptors are en route. They're about one kilometer away. North." God, would these invading aliens ever leave them alone?

"Shit," Marcus bit out. Then he went silent.

She didn't know if he was thinking or fighting. She pictured his rugged, scarred face creased in thought as he formulated a plan.

Then his deep, rasping voice was back. "Elle, we need an escape route and an evac now. Shaw's been hit in the leg, Cruz is carrying him. We can't engage more raptors."

She tapped the screen rapidly, pulling up drone images and archived maps. *Escape route, escape route.* Her mind clicked through the options. She knew Shaw was taller and heavier than Cruz, but the armor they wore had slim-line exoskeletons built into them allowing the soldiers to lift heavier loads and run faster and longer than normal. She tapped the screen again. *Come on.* She needed somewhere safe for a Hawk quadcopter to set down and pick them up.

"Elle? We need it now!"

Just then her comp beeped. She looked at the image and saw a hazy patch of red appear in the broken shell of a nearby building. The heat sensor had detected something else down there. Something big.

Right next to the team.

She touched her ear. "Rex! Marcus, a rex has just woken up in the building beside you."

"Fuck! Get us out of here. Now."

Oh, God. Elle swallowed back bile. Images of rexes, with their huge, dinosaur-like bodies and mouths full of teeth, flashed in her head.

More laser fire ripped through her earpiece and she heard the wild roar of the awakening beast.

Block it out. She focused on the screen. Marcus needed her. The team needed her.

"Run past the rex." One hand curled into a tight fist, her nails cutting into her skin. "Go through its hiding place."

"Through its nest?" Marcus' voice was incredulous. "You know how territorial they are."

"It's the best way out. On the other side you'll find a railway tunnel. Head south along it about eight hundred meters, and you'll find an emergency exit ladder that you can take to the surface. I'll have a Hawk pick you up there."

A harsh expulsion of breath. "Okay, Elle. You've gotten us out of too many tight spots for me to doubt you now."

His words had heat creeping into her cheeks. His praise...it left her giddy. In her life BAI—before alien invasion—no one had valued her opinions. Her father, her mother, even her almost-fiancé, they'd all thought her nothing more than a pretty ornament. Hell, she *had* been a silly, pretty party girl.

And because she'd been inept, her parents were dead. Elle swallowed. A year had passed since that horrible night during the first wave of the alien attack, when their giant ships had appeared in the skies. Her parents had died that night, along with most of the world.

"Hell Squad, ready to go to hell?" Marcus called out.

"Hell, yeah!" the team responded. "The devil needs an ass-kicking!"

"Woo-hoo!" Another voice blasted through her head-set, pulling her from the past. "Ellie, baby, this dirty alien's nest stinks like Cruz's socks. You should be here."

A smile tugged at Elle's lips. Shaw Baird always knew how to ease the tension of a life-or-death situation.

"Oh, yeah, Hell Squad gets the best missions," Shaw added.

Elle watched the screen, her smile slipping. Everyone called Squad Six the Hell Squad. She was never quite sure if it was because they were hellions, or because they got sent into hell to do the toughest, dirtiest missions.

There was no doubt they were a bunch of rebels. Marcus had a rep for not following orders. Just the previous week, he'd led the squad in to destroy a raptor outpost but had detoured to rescue survivors huddled in an abandoned hospital that was under attack. At the debrief, the general's yelling had echoed through the entire base. Marcus, as always, had been silent.

"Shut up, Shaw, you moron." The deep female voice carried an edge.

Elle had decided there were two words that best described the only female soldier on Hell Squad—loner and tough. Claudia Frost was everything Elle wasn't. Elle cleared her throat. "Just get yourselves back to base."

As she listened to the team fight their way through the rex nest, she tapped in the command for one of the Hawk quadcopters to pick them up.

The line crackled. "Okay, Elle, we're through. Heading to the evac point."

Marcus' deep voice flowed over her and the tense muscles in her shoulders relaxed a fraction. They'd be back soon. They were okay. He was okay.

She pressed a finger to the blue dot leading the team. "The bird's en route, Marcus."

"Thanks. See you soon."

She watched on the screen as the large, black shadow of the Hawk hovered above the ground and the team boarded. The rex was headed in their direction, but they were already in the air.

Elle stood and ran her hands down her trousers. She shot a wry smile at the camouflage fabric. It felt like a dream to think that she'd ever owned a very expensive, designer wardrobe. And heels—God, how long had it been since she'd worn heels? These days, fatigues were all that hung in her closet. Well-worn ones, at that.

As she headed through the tunnels of the underground base toward the landing pads, she forced herself not to run. She'd see him—them—soon enough. She rounded a corner and almost collided with someone.

"General. Sorry, I wasn't watching where I was going."

"No problem, Elle." General Adam Holmes had a military-straight bearing he'd developed in the United Coalition Army and a head of dark hair with a brush of distinguished gray at his temples. He was classically handsome, and his eyes were a piercing blue. He was the top man in this last little outpost of humanity. "Squad Six on their way back?"

"Yes, sir." They fell into step.

"And they secured the map?"

God, Elle had almost forgotten about the map. "Ah, yes. They got images of it just before they came under attack by raptors."

"Well, let's go welcome them home. That map might just be the key to the fate of mankind."

They stepped into the landing areas. Staff in various military uniforms and civilian clothes raced around. After the raptors had attacked, bringing all manner of vicious creatures with them to take over the Earth, what was left of mankind had banded together.

Whoever had survived now lived here in an underground base in the Blue Mountains, just west of Sydney, or in the other, similar outposts scattered across the planet. All arms of the United Coalition's military had been decimated. In the early days, many of the surviving soldiers had fought amongst themselves, trying to work out who outranked whom. But it didn't take long before General Holmes had unified everyone against the aliens. Most squads were a mix of ranks and experience, but the teams eventually worked themselves out. Most didn't even bother with titles and rank anymore.

Sirens blared, followed by the clang of metal. Huge doors overhead retracted into the roof.

A Hawk filled the opening, with its sleek gray body and four spinning rotors. It was near-silent, running on a small thermonuclear engine. It turned slowly as it descended to the landing pad.

Her team was home.

She threaded her hands together, her heart beating a little faster.

Marcus was home.

Marcus Steele wanted a shower and a beer.

Hot, sweaty and covered in raptor blood, he leaped down from the Hawk and waved at his team to follow. He kept a sharp eye on the medical team who raced out to tend to Shaw. Dr. Emerson Green was leading them, her white lab coat snapping around her curvy body. The blonde doctor caught his gaze and tossed him a salute.

Shaw was cursing and waving them off, but one look from Marcus and the lanky Australian sniper shut his mouth.

Marcus swung his laser carbine over his shoulder and scraped a hand down his face. Man, he'd kill for a hot shower. Of course, he'd have to settle for a cold one since they only allowed hot water for two hours in the morning in order to conserve energy. But maybe after that beer he'd feel human again.

"Well done, Squad Six." Holmes stepped forward. "Steele, I hear you got images of the map."

Holmes might piss Marcus off sometimes, but at least the guy always got straight to the point. He was a general to the bone and always looked spit and polish. Everything about him screamed money and a fancy education, so not surprisingly, he tended to rub the troops the wrong way.

Marcus pulled the small, clear comp chip from his pocket. "We got it."

Then he spotted her.

Shit. It was always a small kick in his chest. His gaze traveled up Elle Milton's slim figure, coming to rest on a face he could stare at all day. She wasn't very tall, but that didn't matter. Something about her high cheekbones, pale-blue eyes, full lips, and rain of chocolate-brown hair...it all worked for him. Perfectly. She was beautiful, kind, and far too good to be stuck in this crappy under-ground maze of tunnels, dressed in hand-me-down fatigues.

She raised a slim hand. Marcus shot her a small nod.

"Hey, Ellie-girl. Gonna give me a kiss?"

Shaw passed on an iono-stretcher hovering off the ground and Marcus gritted his teeth. The tall, blond sniper with his lazy charm and Aussie drawl was popular with the ladies. Shaw flashed his killer smile at Elle.

She smiled back, her blue eyes twinkling and Marcus' gut cramped.

Then she put one hand on her hip and gave the sniper a head-to-toe look. She shook her head. "I think you get enough kisses."

Marcus released the breath he didn't realize he was holding.

"See you later, Sarge." Zeke Jackson slapped Marcus on the back and strolled past. His usually-silent twin, Gabe, was beside him. The twins, both former Coalition Army Special Forces soldiers, were deadly in the field. Marcus was damned happy to have them on his squad.

"Howdy, Princess." Claudia shot Elle a smirk as she passed.

Elle rolled her eyes. "Claudia."

Cruz, Marcus' second-in-command and best friend from their days as Coalition Marines, stepped up beside Marcus and crossed his arms over his chest. He'd already pulled some of his lightweight body armor off, and the ink on his arms was on display.

The general nodded at Cruz before looking back at Marcus. "We need Shaw back up and running ASAP. If the raptor prisoner we interrogated is correct, that map shows one of the main raptor communications hubs." There was a blaze of excitement in the usually-stoic general's voice. "It links all their operations together."

Yeah, Marcus knew it was big. Destroy the hub, send the raptor operations into disarray.

The general continued. "As soon as the tech team can break the encryption on the chip and give us a location for the raptor comms hub—" his piercing gaze leveled on Marcus "—I want your team back out there to plant the bomb."

Marcus nodded. He knew if they destroyed the raptors' communications it gave humanity a fighting chance. A chance they desperately needed.

He traded a look with Cruz. Looked like they were going out to wade through raptor gore again sooner than anticipated.

Man, he really wanted that beer.

Then Marcus' gaze landed on Elle again. He didn't keep going out there for himself, or Holmes. He went so people like Elle and the other civilian survivors had a chance. A chance to do more than simply survive.

"Shaw's wound is minor. Doc Emerson should have him good as new in an hour or so." Since the advent of the nano-meds, simple wounds could be healed in hours, rather than days and weeks. They carried a dose of the microscopic medical machines on every mission, but only for dire emergencies. The nano-meds had to be administered and monitored by professionals or they were just as likely to kill you from the inside than heal you.

General Holmes nodded. "Good."

Elle cleared her throat. "There's no telling how long it will take to break the encryption. I've been working with the tech team and even if they break it, we may not be able to translate it all. We're getting better at learning the raptor language but there are still huge amounts of it we don't yet understand."

Marcus' jaw tightened. There was always something. He knew Noah Kim—their resident genius computer specialist—and his geeks were good, but if they couldn't read the damn raptor language...

Holmes turned. "Steele, let your team have some downtime and be ready the minute Noah has anything."

"Yes, sir." As the general left, Marcus turned to Cruz. "Go get yourself a beer, Ramos."

"Don't need to tell me more than once, *amigo*. I would kill for some of my dad's tamales to go with it." Something sad flashed across a face all the women in the base mooned over, then he grimaced and a bone-deep weariness colored his words. "Need to wash the raptor off me, first." He tossed Marcus a casual salute, Elle a smile, and strode out.

Marcus frowned after his friend and absently started loosening his body armor.

Elle moved up beside him. "I can take the comp chip to Noah."

"Sure." He handed it to her. When her fingers brushed his he felt the warmth all the way through him. Hell, he had it bad. Thankfully, he still had his armor on or she'd see his cock tenting his pants.

"I'll come find you as soon as we have something." She glanced up at him. Smiled. "Are you going to rec night tonight? I hear Cruz might even play guitar for us."

The Friday-night gathering was a chance for everyone to blow off a bit of steam and drink too much homebrewed beer. And Cruz had an unreal talent with a guitar, although lately Marcus hadn't seen the man play too much.

Marcus usually made an appearance at these parties, then left early to head back to his room to study raptor movements or plan the squad's next missions. "Yeah, I'll be there."

"Great." She smiled. "I'll see you there, then." She hurried out clutching the chip.

He stared at the tunnel where she'd exited for a long while after she disappeared, and finally ripped his chest armor off. Ah, on second thought, maybe going to the rec night wasn't a great idea. Watching her pretty face and captivating smile would drive him crazy. He cursed under his breath. He really needed that cold shower.

As he left the landing pads, he reminded himself he should be thinking of the mission. Destroy the hub and kill more aliens. Rinse and repeat. Death and killing, that was about all he knew.

He breathed in and caught a faint trace of Elle's floral scent. She was clean and fresh and good. She always worried about them, always had a smile, and she was damned good at providing their comms and intel.

She was why he fought through the muck every day. So she could live and the goodness in her would survive. She deserved more than blood and death and killing.

And she sure as hell deserved more than a battled-scarred, bloodstained soldier.

Hell Squad
Marcus
Cruz

Gabe

Reed

Roth

Noah

Shaw

Holmes

Niko

Finn

Theron

Hemi

Ash

Levi

Also Available as Audiobooks!

PREVIEW - AMONG GALACTIC RUINS

MORE ACTION ROMANCE?

**ACTION
ADVENTURE
TREASURE HUNTS
SEXY SCI-FI ROMANCE**

When astro-archeologist and museum curator Dr. Lexa Carter discovers a secret map to a lost old Earth treasure— a priceless Fabergé egg—she's excited at the prospect of a treasure hunt to the dangerous desert planet of Zerzura. What she's not so happy about is being saddled with a bodyguard—the museum's mysterious new head of security, Damon Malik.

After many dangerous years as a galactic spy, Damon

Malik just wanted a quiet job where no one tried to kill him. Instead of easy work in a museum full of artifacts, he finds himself on a backwater planet babysitting the most infuriating woman he's ever met.

She thinks he's arrogant. He thinks she's a trouble-magnet. But among the desert sands and ruins, adventure led by a young, brash treasure hunter named Dathan Phoenix, takes a deadly turn. As it becomes clear that someone doesn't want them to find the treasure, Lexa and Damon will have to trust each other just to survive.

The Phoenix Adventures

Among Galactic Ruins
At Star's End
In the Devil's Nebula
On a Rogue Planet
Beneath a Trojan Moon
Beyond Galaxy's Edge
On a Cyborg Planet
Return to Dark Earth
On a Barbarian World
Lost in Barbarian Space
Through Uncharted Space
Crashed on an Ice World

Marcus

Cruz

Gabe

Reed

Roth

Noah

Shaw

Holmes

Niko

Finn

Theron

Hemi

Ash

Levi

Also Available as Audiobooks!

The Anomaly Series

Time Thief

Mind Raider

Soul Stealer

Salvation

Anomaly Series Box Set

The Phoenix Adventures

Among Galactic Ruins

At Star's End

In the Devil's Nebula

On a Rogue Planet

Beneath a Trojan Moon

Beyond Galaxy's Edge

On a Cyborg Planet

Return to Dark Earth

On a Barbarian World

Lost in Barbarian Space

Through Uncharted Space

Crashed on an Ice World

Perma Series

Winter Fusion

A Galactic Holiday

Warriors of the Wind

Tempest

Storm & Seduction

Fury & Darkness

Standalone Titles

Savage Dragon

Hunter's Surrender

One Night with the Wolf

For more information visit AnnaHackettBooks.com

ABOUT THE AUTHOR

I'm a USA Today bestselling author and I'm passionate about ***action romance***. I love stories that combine the thrill of falling in love with the excitement of action, danger and adventure. I'm a sucker for that moment when the team is walking in slow motion, shoulder-to-shoulder heading off into battle. I write about people overcoming unbeatable odds and achieving seemingly impossible goals. I like to believe it's possible for all of us to do the same.

My books are mixture of action, adventure and sexy romance and they're recommended for anyone who enjoys fast-paced stories where the boy wins the girl at the end (or sometimes the girl wins the boy!)

For release dates, action romance info, free books, and other fun stuff, sign up for the latest news here:

Website: www.annahackettbooks.com

Printed in Great Britain
by Amazon